Under Covers

D1113290

Rhonda Bowen

Copyright © 2015 by Rhonda Bowen

ISBN: 150880026X

ISBN-13: 978-1508800262

Dedication

For the special women I know and those I don't who have chosen to be free and the people who love them.

"Therefore if any man be in Christ, he is a new creature: old things are passed away; behold all things are become new."

2 Corinthians 5:17

Chapter One

The first sign was the milk. The glass bottle hit the ground as soon as she opened the fridge door. It shattered into a thousand pieces. Naomi's body went still. She watched the white fluid seep through her toes and spread across the floor while the feeling of dread seeped over her stomach.

Her mother always had a thing about milk. She said the milk had been sour the morning Naomi's grandfather died. The creamer had leaked all over the fridge the day her cousin, Marika, lost her baby. And even Naomi, who was usually the more practical one, couldn't forget the fly she found floating peacefully in the saucer of white liquid the night before she lost her job at Whisper. Bad milk was a bad sign – especially the week of your wedding.

Naomi shut the bad thoughts out of her mind even as she pushed the fridge door closed and grabbed the paper towels off the kitchen counter to clean up the mess. She was being silly. Nothing would go wrong with the wedding. She and Jordan had been planning this day for the past six months. She had checked everything twice, some things three times. And what she hadn't caught, her wedding planner/sister-in-law-to-be, Amanda had. So, she was covered. Naomi didn't believe her family's silly old wives' tales anyway.

Still, she took several deep breaths to calm her racing heart. The phone rang and jolted her back to reality.

"Girl, where are you?" Natasha hollered through the phone. She didn't wait for Naomi to say hello. "Ryan Lue just brought over the proofs from the shoot. I hope you didn't get all bridezilla and forget about this."

5

Naomi heard shuffling and movement in the background and figured that her co-editor was already busy juggling a million tasks at the office even though it was only 9:15am. It would also explain why Naomi was on speakerphone even though Natasha knew she hated it.

"No, I didn't forget," Naomi cradled the phone between her ear and her shoulder. She rushed out of the kitchen back to her tiny bedroom to get dressed. Clearly, breakfast would have to be sacrificed. "I'm just getting ready to leave now."

"Good, cause I don't have your eye," Natasha murmured. "I can't pick these without you."

"Yes, you can," Naomi said as she tried to pull on her dress without losing grip of the phone. "I've seen you do it myself."

"Yeah but you were always standing behind me, breathing down my neck," Natasha said with a laugh.

Naomi stood on her tiptoes in her closet. She reached for one of her Aldo shoe boxes. It almost landed on her head along with several other objects as it came crashing down.

"How about I was standing behind you supporting you?" Naomi picked through the pile for her plum wedges. "Preparing you for the day when I would get married and go on my honeymoon for two weeks, while you held it down at Street Life."

"Yeah, yeah," Natasha murmured, not convinced. "Just get your behind over here. I'm drowning."

"I'll be there in ten minutes."

Naomi tossed the cordless on the bed, wiggled into her shoes and grabbed her purse. She was about to dash out of the room when the cloth covered notebook on the ground near the shoeboxes caught her eye. Apprehension made her pause for a second. She walked over. The scrawl of her

6

handwriting on the open pages drew her eye, but she picked up the notebook and closed it before she could read any of the words. She didn't need that this morning. Not on top of everything else. She stuffed it in the empty shoe box and chucked the box back on the top shelf of her closet.

Naomi dashed out the bedroom towards the front door. She wasn't in such a hurry that she didn't notice the few drops of milk beside the fridge she had missed. First the milk, then the notebook. This was not how she wanted to start her morning.

"Nothing bad is going to happen," she said out loud, though there was no one else to hear her. All the same, she ran back to the kitchen and grabbed another paper towel. She hoped to the heavens she was right. The kitchen spill had been wiped away, but Naomi couldn't wipe away the unsettling feeling that things were about to change – and not for the better.

Chapter Two

"Okay, okay I'm here," Naomi announced as the elevator opened on the top floor of the converted brownstone that housed Street Life magazine. "Update me."

Before she could take two steps, she was surrounded.

"J. Cole's people have still not gotten back to us about approving the quotes in the article," David squeezed his ever-present blue stress ball as he walked beside her. "It's been almost a week."

"Email Connie and tell her if we don't hear back from them by lunch, we're pulling the article and using Drake on the cover instead," Naomi made her way through the maze of desks that sat in the open floor plan, office space.

"Wait, I thought we were still in development with the piece on Drake?" the young features writer asked confused.

"We are, but she doesn't know that," Naomi winked. "Next?"

An assistant shoved a pen and a couple sheets of paper with fluorescent arrow stickers on them into Naomi's hands. "We need you to sign off on the deposit for the Hilton Ballroom in November," the wiry young woman kept pace with Naomi.

"How are the plans for the new online platform launch going?" Naomi asked as she flipped through the documents. She scribbled her signature.

"Venue and catering are booked. Gina's people are trying to squeeze us on decor but when I told her the Hilton offered to cover all of that for us, she changed her tune,"

8

Hannah smirked.

"Nice," Naomi handed back the documents. "Keep me updated via email while I'm gone."

"Oh and someone from Ilana Baranoski's office called again," Hannah added. She handed Naomi a sticky note with the details.

"Thanks." Naomi took the note. She crushed it in her hand without looking at it. "Brock, what do you have for me?"

The crowd had begun to thin as she collected reports and signed off on more documents.

"Urban Decor wants four full pages near the center to showcase their new Nicki Minaj line."

Naomi let out a laugh. "Nicki Minaj designs home furnishings now?"

"Apparently," Brock pursed his lips. "They say its urban style meets New York living."

"I'll bet," Naomi paused at the bottom of the stairs that would take her up to the second level. "They can have one center page and half a page near the back."

"They're willing to sign a six month advertising contract for that amount of space every month," Andre said. "That's a lot of guaranteed revenue."

"Yeah and next month they'll be pushing Lil Kim's nursery decor. They can forget it. This is an urban culture magazine, not a hip hop shopping catalog." Naomi turned to head up the exposed steel, winding staircase.

Brock chuckled. "You're the boss."

She shook her head as she entered Natasha's office at the top of the stairs. With the open layout of the two-level office building, she had been able to see her second-in-charge. Natasha had taken up residence at the railing and waited impatiently for her the minute Naomi stepped off the elevator.

"Did you hear about this Nicki Minaj home decor thing?" Naomi asked as she dropped her purse and documents in the chair near the door.

"No, but I am sure it will be over by the time our next issue goes to print," Natasha responded absently as she shuffled around glossies on the ten foot glass layout table near the center of the office. "Come look at these. We need to submit by noon and we haven't done the captions yet."

Naomi slipped her sunset orange frames on her face to take a better look. The images would be perfect for the magazine. Ryan Lue had done a great job. She was glad they had hired him to go out to North Carolina and do the shoot with J. Cole instead of using submitted press shots from his representatives. If they played their cards right, they could even get some revenue off the images, particularly the shots from inside his new home, which up until recently had not been seen by the public.

"So I was thinking these six for the inside and this one for the cover," Natasha tagged several photos with stickies.

Naomi bit her lip as she scanned the options before her. "Yes, yes, yes, no and yes," she confirmed most of Natasha's choices.

"You were thinking of this shot for the inside page beside the article right?" Naomi tapped a photo with the artist sitting on the edge of a rusted subway car with snow covering the edges of the scene.

"Yeah," Natasha said. "Reminds me of 1996 hip-hop. You know, back when it was good. It kind of fits the article."

Naomi nodded. "Switch it with the one you chose for the cover and use this instead. Put the dumpster fire shot on the inside."

Natasha nodded. "You know, I thought that at first. Then I switched it."

Naomi headed back to the chair to retrieve her things. "Stop doubting your gut, Natasha. You're good at this. You need me for anything else?"

"No," Natasha murmured, as she retagged the photos. "Not while your man is waiting for you in your office."

Naomi backed towards the door. "He's here?"

"Yes," Natasha's lips cracked into a smile as she heard the delight in her boss and friend's voice. "For about twenty minutes now. So you better not keep him waiting any longer."

Naomi heard that.

She slipped out of the office and down the corridor to her own space. Jordan must have heard her voice. He leaned lazily against the door frame, looking better in a collared shirt and jeans than the photo-shopped image of a bare-chested J. Cole that she had seen just moments earlier. Naomi felt the heat begin at her toes and travel all the way through her as their eyes locked.

How had she gotten this lucky?

"Good morning, Red." His eyes devoured her as the distance closed between them.

"Good morning."

He pulled her into his arms. Naomi sank into him willingly as he parted her smiling lips with his.

"Babe, the whole office can see us," she murmured against his delicious mouth.

"Good." He kissed her again. "Let them see what Black love looks like."

She heard a hoot and a few whistles from the level

below.

"Yeah, but I don't like to share."

He chuckled as she pulled him into her office and tipped the door closed behind them. She kissed him one last time, and then buried herself in his embrace. She inhaled his scent of sandalwood and urban man as she pressed her face against his chest and mentally counted down the days until she could wake up wrapped in that scent every morning. A girl could hardly keep her clothes on at the thought.

"Missed me, did you?" he asked softly into her hair.

"Like the breeze on a hot day." She tilted her head back to look at him. "You are never allowed to go away for that long again."

Jordan stroked her cheeks with his thumbs as he cupped her face. "Two weeks is a long time. At least next time it's that long, you'll be with me."

"Next time, and the rest of our lives." Naomi gazed into his eyes.

"And the rest of our lives," he echoed. They looked at each other for a long time. After four years, it felt like they could read each other's thoughts.

Naomi untangled herself from his embrace and eased him into her high back leather chair. "How was the meeting? You sounded so down when I spoke to you before you left. I didn't know if it was just fatigue or something else."

As a buyer for hotels, Jordan's job took him all over North America and occasionally to different parts of the world to negotiate the wholesale purchase of furniture and decor for new resorts and hotels or for older chains looking to remodel or renovate. He had recently travelled to China to negotiate the purchase and shipping of items for a new Ramada hotel opening just outside New York City.

"It turned out pretty well in the end," he said as he pulled her onto his lap. "It was a lot of travelling but we were able to hammer down a good deal with the supplier. I think I am going to like working with this manufacturer. They have good quality products and the workers at their factories seem to be treated pretty well."

Naomi raised an eyebrow. "Does that mean I get to go to China?"

He grinned. "Maybe. How's your Mandarin?"

"Rusty," she said. "As in virtually useless."

Jordan chuckled and dropped a kiss on her cheek. "Have lunch with me later."

She pouted. "Can't. The girls have this whole afternoon planned. Lunch, then the spa, then some last minute wedding stuff."

He rolled his eyes. "This sounds like an Amanda kind of plan."

Naomi laughed. "It is, but don't hate on her. She's probably more excited about this wedding than both of us. You know your sister can't wait for you to get married."

"You know why right?" he asked. "So mom will have one more person to bug about giving her grandkids."

"Ain't nothin' wrong with that," Naomi wiggled her eyebrows.

His smile widened. She couldn't help but laugh. Even though Jordan tried to act cool, she knew he was dying to have kids.

She felt her shoulder vibrate and slipped her fingers into his shirt pocket to pull out his phone. Naomi glanced at the screen then handed it to him.

"It's work."

He answered the call without moving. "This is Jordan...yes, they're ready to ship next week. The contracts are with Jeff. Go ahead and prepare the payment and I will sign the requisition when I get into the office...okay...see you soon."

He ended the call, rested his head back and closed his eyes.

"Gotta go?"

"Mhmm," he murmured, his eyes still closed.

Naomi rested her head on his shoulder. "Think our lives will let us leave for the two weeks of our honeymoon?"

"I'm not sure," he said.

She sat up. "Maybe we could stage a kidnapping."

"Ramada would pay the ransom and deduct it from my fee."

Naomi snorted. "You're probably right. You should go then."

She gave him room to stand and followed him to the door.

Naomi leaned against the door jam. "Squeeze me in for dinner? I'll find a way to dodge your sister if I have to."

"It's a deal." Jordan stole a kiss then slipped away. She watched as he walked his fine self down the stairs and towards the elevator. She noticed a lot of her female staff watched too, including Natasha.

"What you looking at?" she called down the corridor.

"Girl, you know what I'm looking at." Natasha gave Naomi a pointed look. She shook her head. "You sure he doesn't have any brothers?"

Naomi laughed and waved to Jordan as he got into the elevator. When the doors closed she glanced down at the action below. The bees were busy working. They were a small hive but a productive one. When Street Life first started out as an online publication, it had just been Naomi, Natasha and a rolodex of old journalism contacts, freelancers and photographers whom they could pull in on an as needed basis. Now, six years later, the magazine was going strong on all social media platforms. It also enjoyed a strong circulation in most of the major North American markets. That meant that their team of two had become a team of twelve.

Naomi was grateful for the success of what had started out as a side hobby for her and her friend, but sometimes the knowledge of how many people depended on her made her panic. Today was one of those days. She took a deep breath and stepped to the railing.

"Okay listen up." Movement stopped as all eyes turned to look at her. "As you guys know, today is my last day before I go off and marry that gorgeous man that just walked out of here."

Naomi grinned at the cheers and whistles she received.

"While I am gone, Natasha is going to run the ship, which she is more than capable of doing," Naomi said with a smile as she glanced over at her friend. "She does it most of the time anyway. But if you absolutely need me, I'll be here in office until 1:30 so get in where you fit in while you can. That is all."

Naomi turned towards her door even as the movement started downstairs. She knew that she would spend most of the next four hours hand holding her staff, but that was fine with her. Everything major that needed to be done was already taken care of or passed off to Natasha, so she had the time.

"You're still doing the whole afternoon thing with Amanda and Charlie?" Natasha followed Naomi into her office.

"*WE* are doing the whole afternoon thing," Naomi sunk down into her chair and opened up her laptop. "You know I need you to help me navigate those two."

"So we're both going to ditch the office this afternoon?" Natasha asked, her eyebrow rose. "Think the kids can manage without us?"

"They're old enough," Naomi pulled up some documents. "By the way, Camille was supposed to be there too but she was going to call me back for the location. Have you heard anything from her?"

"No, but I'll text her the details," Natasha retrieved her Blackberry out of her back pocket, just as a knock sounded at the door.

"Come in, David," Naomi waved him inside. "Connie called back, didn't she?"

"In less than ten minutes," David said with a grin.

Naomi laughed. It was going to be a busy four hours.

Chapter Three

"Yes! Yes! Right there! Oh yes! That's it...that's it exactly."

"Girl, you need to stop with all that," Natasha said, her voice sounded muffled as it floated up from a foot above the floor. "People are going to think something freaky is going on in here."

After lunch, Amanda had taken Naomi and the other girls to the Cornelia Day Resort where they received the full bridal package. They had done a quick body treatment and then massages. The next round would be a skin soak and facial. Naomi couldn't remember the last time she had been so pampered. Though the weekend getaway at a luxury resort Jordan had given her for her thirty-second birthday last month came pretty close.

"What's freaky is the way my muscles have melted under this massage," Charlie murmured from her similar face down position. "Aleksi, whatever they pay you at this place, I'll double it if you come work for me."

The Russian massage therapist chuckled and continued to press his hands into Charlie's bare shoulders.

"There you go again, Charlie. You think you can buy people onto your side," Amanda commented from her own massage bed. "Not everyone has a price tag."

"Of course they do. You just have to keep going higher until you find it," Charlie quipped. "Isn't that right, Naomi?"

"Uh-uh. Y'all leave me out of this. I am too relaxed right now to get drawn into other people's arguments. It's been a long time since my body's felt this good," Naomi said.

17

"What? Jordan's not taking care of that?" Charlie said cheekily. "What you marrying him for then?"

"Eww! I am right here!" Amanda said with a shudder. "I do not need that mental picture of my brother."

"I am marrying him because I love him," Naomi replied. "Because he is the best thing that ever happened to me, and because he loves me. I think that's good enough."

"I do too," Natasha said. "Everything else is none of anyone else's business."

"Agreed," Amanda said so enthusiastically that Naomi and Natasha both started laughing.

Charlie scoffed. "You guys are no fun."

"No, you're just too nosy," Natasha said. "Get your own man and stop nosing around other people's. And by your own, I don't mean that ratchet mess you brought to the engagement party."

"Ouch," Amanda murmured.

"Owen is not a ratchet mess. He's a wonderful guy," Charlie responded, not the least bit miffed.

"He's married..."

"Separated," Charlie corrected. "And we're just hanging out."

Natasha snorted. "Okay, Alicia Keyes. Whatever you and Swizz B. need to tell yourselves to sleep at night."

Naomi closed her eyes and tuned out her two friends. If she didn't know better she would think those two hated each other. But she did know better. The three of them had grown up together in New Jersey. Since they were ten years old, they had went to the same schools and slept over at each other's homes. In fact, when it was time to start Street Life magazine, all three of them had put in the capital necessary to get it going. Charlie opted to be a silent partner. Naomi knew they never would have been able to get things off the ground without Charlie's input and she was always thankful to her for that.

They had always been pretty close, until three years ago when Charlie had suddenly decided she wanted to sell her stock in Street Life at a time when neither Naomi nor Natasha could afford to buy it back. Naomi had to put her house on the market and go back to renting. Natasha had to borrow money from her family to make it happen. Naomi didn't really mind selling her first home because it required more of her than she initially anticipated when she purchased it. But Natasha had not gotten over the way Charlie had stretched them thin. Her relationship with Charlie had been tenuous at best since then.

Still, they were the closest women to Naomi and she couldn't imagine getting married without either of them. In fact, she kind of owed Charlie because she had been the one to introduce Jordan and Naomi at a barbeque for the board members of the Thirty Under Thirty Awards. It was a fact Charlie rarely let her forget.

"Nay-Nay, you really gonna let her do me like that the week of your wedding?" Charlie asked. "After all, if I hadn't introduced you to Mr. Lennox, we wouldn't even be here right now."

"Actually, you all wouldn't be here if it wasn't for me," Amanda said. "None of you even knew this oasis existed before I pulled up to the entrance."

"Very true," Naomi said. "Props to the sister-in-law."

"Thank you," Amanda said. She sounded pleased. "But if I knew your sister would be this late, I would have booked for four instead of five. Where is Camille?"

"That's the million dollar question," Naomi said. "I have called her all morning and nothing."

"She didn't text me back either," Natasha said. "When was the last time you spoke to her?"

"Two days ago," Naomi said. "She was finishing up a paper she needed to submit before the end of the semester. I know she was a little stressed out over it but I don't know why she would just fall off the grid like that."

"Are you worried?" Amanda asked.

Naomi didn't answer right away. All morning, after every unanswered call from Camille, something heavy had settled in the pit of Naomi's stomach but she had tried to ignore it.

"Don't be," Charlie said. "You know Camille. Always disappearing deep into something. She's twenty-one, what do you expect? She probably pulled an all-nighter to hand in her paper, then partied with her friends. I bet she crashed, dead asleep at her dorm or at your mom's..."

"...or with that boyfriend of hers," Natasha said dryly.

"Yeah, I meant to say something about that," Amanda said as they sat up from the massages and put on their robes. "I had an odd feeling about him at the engagement party. He's a tad creepy."

"Who, Andre? Why?" Charlie flipped her long dark hair over her shoulder as she turned to frown at Amanda. "Cause he's not New York royalty like the rest of your clan?"

"No," Amanda said defensively. "It's just...I just got a weird feeling that's all."

"No, I know what you mean," Naomi slipped on the plush spa slippers as she pulled the belt on her robe tighter. "I don't know much about him. But I'm not too fond of him either."

Something about Camille's latest boy toy made Naomi uneasy. There was a hardness about him. An edge. He reminded Naomi of her own brother. And that scared

Naomi in more ways than she cared to think about.

"I don't know," Natasha said. "He was pretty polite during the evening. He stayed close to Camille..."

"...or smothered her." Amanda said as she led the way out of the massage room. "I didn't even know she was seeing someone. If I had known, I wouldn't have invited my nephew-in-law to meet her. I thought they would have hit it off."

"That little light-skinned cutie was your husband's nephew?" Charlie asked, the interest in her voice obvious.

"Down girl, he is way too young for your cougar behind," Natasha glanced behind her at Charlie.

"Then someone should have told him, cause I couldn't get rid of him all night," Charlie said with a grin. "Besides, I think thirty-three is too young to be a cougar."

Naomi answered Amanda's initial question. "She just started seeing him a couple months ago. She met him at some campus event. Although, he doesn't exactly strike me as university material."

"Now that, I can't argue with," Charlie said knowingly. Though Camille's boyfriend had been pretty quiet, the scars on his face, tattoos and hood-life aura suggested a lot.

Naomi rubbed her arms. She felt chilled all of sudden. "I just hope this one passes as swiftly as the last couple of them."

"Ladies! I hope you have enjoyed your treatment thus far."

The tall blonde who served as their host for the afternoon stood just outside the doors of the massage area. She smiled serenely at them.

"Yes, we have." Naomi smiled. "It's been amazing."

The other women murmured their agreement.

"Excellent," the host clasped her hands together. "Then let's continue, shall we?"

"Up next is our Zen ginseng facial treatment and milk bath. Both are designed to soften, moisturize and replenish your skin, making it supple and giving you a fresh, healthy glow."

"Milk bath," Natasha murmured to Naomi. "Fancy, fancy. I am going to enjoy having you married into the family of a former New York governor. The perks are amazing."

Naomi chuckled and followed her friends through a wide archway into a covered garden area. Beautiful flowers and lush thick foliage surrounded six stone beds built into the ground. They were filled with a pure white milky liquid.

The host had said, "Well ladies, go ahead. In a few minutes our beauty therapists will come in and begin applying your facial masks."

Then she disappeared into the main building. The four women looked at each other curiously.

Naomi grinned. "Well, who's going first?".

"You're the bride," Natasha folded her arms.

"Amanda, this was your idea," Naomi looked over at her friend.

Amanda rolled her eyes. "The lengths I have to go through to get you all to try something new."

Amanda disrobed and slipped down into the milk bath. She let out a deep sigh as she laid her head back on the headrest.

"You sold me, " Charlie followed suit.

Within minutes, they all soaked in the warm creamy liquid. Although it felt a little strange, Naomi had to admit it also felt really great. She had heard about milk baths before, but this was the first time she'd ever experienced one personally. She really wished Camille were here. She would have gotten a kick out of all of this. Growing up with a mother who had migrated from Trinidad to New York, Naomi had known what it was like to struggle. Her mother often worked two or three jobs. She left Naomi to learn how to take care of herself from very early on, and later when Camille arrived, she had to take care of her too. Though Naomi's brother was six years older than her, his adjustment to life in the USA had been a harder transition for him at age sixteen than it had been for Naomi as a ten year old. He had been too caught up in his own issues to be around much for her. And then after a while, he wasn't around at all.

Naomi's thoughts began to cloud over as her mind wondered to Nigel. Some days she felt like she hadn't known him at all, and other days she feared that she was nothing more than a hare's breath away from being just like him. They had grown up the exact same way and yet were so different, or so Naomi liked to tell herself. Maybe they weren't really that different after all. Maybe your gene pool condemned you to certain destinies and there was nothing you could do about it. Look at Camille. She had the least contact with Nigel out of all of them and yet their personalities, their approach to life was so similar it sometimes kept Naomi awake at night, and kept her tense with worry. Kind of like she was right now.

Naomi sat up and reached for her robe, abandoned on the marble next to her soaker. "Maybe I should call her again."

Natasha reached over and grabbed Naomi's hand before she got to her cell phone in the robe's pocket.

"Relax, Nay-Nay. This whole spa afternoon is for you. Don't spend it worried about Camille."

"I can't help it," Naomi closed her eyes and rested her palm on her forehead. "I hate when she does this. She knows she should call. Or at least send a text message. Something to let me know what's going on."

"Yes, she knows," Natasha said. "And if she wanted to be in touch, she would. But this is how Camille is. This is how she's always been. Getting worked up about it hasn't changed her in the past and it won't now."

"At least I'll know where she is."

"That's assuming she even answers," Natasha argued. "Given that she hasn't bothered to the last seven times you called, I don't think she will now."

"Just give her some space, Nay-Nay," Charlie said from two baths down. "Remember how we were at that age? You gotta give her some room to breathe. Let her make her own choices and deal with the consequences. Let her go."

Naomi let out a deep breath and sank back into the bath. "You're right. I just need to give her some room. I'm sure she'll call tonight. She probably just...forgot."

As she closed her eyes and laid her head back, she tried to let go of her anxiety. Everything would be fine. She worried way too much.

"Ugh! What is that!"

Three pairs of eyes popped open and turned towards Amanda, whose face was twisted in disgust.

"What's that in your bath, Naomi?"

Naomi followed Amanda's eyes to the foot of her bath. Her throat began to close when she saw what her friend exclaimed about. A small black pool infected the creamy white liquid near where her feet should be. Naomi couldn't tell where it came from. It was almost as if it had floated to the top of the liquid from somewhere underneath, but it slowly spread out from the darkest point, like a drop of ink on a damp cloth.

Naomi scrambled back and out over the edge of the stone bath. She scraped her bare legs along the way as cold dread poured through her.

"Something's wrong," she gasped.

"Something's definitely wrong," Amanda said outraged as she stood up. "This is disgusting. I am getting a manager."

"No, no," Naomi shook her head as her eyes stayed glued to the infected liquid. "Something bad...something very, very bad!"

She didn't notice the look Charlie and Natasha exchanged as they pulled on their own robes, but she did catch the grim look in Charlie's eyes as she looked at Naomi. They knew her. They knew that worry was one thing but panic was something entirely different, and she didn't panic for nothing.

"What do you want to do?"

Naomi stared at the tainted image, but all her mind saw was what she had ignored that morning before she left home. All the signs that something was off that she had brushed aside. Maybe they were old wives' tales. Maybe they weren't. But right now there was too much coincidence for it to just be nothing.

"Camille." She got up, grabbed her robe, and hastily pulled it over her barely clad body. "I need to find Camille now."

Chapter Four

Camille was not in her dorm.

In fact, the resident assistant for the dorm had informed Naomi that Camille had already moved out for the summer. A quick glance into her empty room confirmed that she was indeed gone and not coming back.

"Did she tell you she was checking out?" Charlie asked.

"No," Naomi answered as they pulled up to the front of Naomi's mother's home.

The only thing Camille had told Naomi was that she would be staying in the dorm during the summer while she redid a couple courses she had failed the semester before. The check that Naomi had given her to cover the extra dorm expense had already been cashed. She tried not to think about where Camille and that money actually were.

"Okay, let's try not to panic Momma Savoy," Natasha said before they got out of the car. "She has had enough to deal with."

Naomi nodded. She was glad they had convinced Amanda to handle things at the spa and the final wedding prep. She wouldn't have understood this part of Naomi's world anyway. Amanda was all Manhattan and Long Island. New Jersey - especially the part where Naomi grew up - was a long way away from Amanda's world.

The drive to South Trenton, New Jersey, from Fordham University took a little over an hour. During that time, Naomi talked herself down from her hysteria. She was still convinced that something was terribly wrong, but at least she had a plan. If Camille wasn't here, she would search her

26

room and find the address for that worthless scum of a man Camille had hooked up with. She was certain that he was involved in this somehow. She didn't know how she knew, but she did. Call it a sixth sense.

"Momma!" Naomi pushed through the three foot metal gate and hurried up the cracked walkway to the house she had grown up in. There were more Puerto Ricans than Blacks in this neighborhood, which was part of the reason her mother had chosen it. It should have helped keep Nigel, Naomi and Camille out of trouble. But it seemed like trouble looked for them wherever they were.

The front door opened before Naomi got to it. A tired looking older woman in a worn gray pantsuit stood in the entryway.

Naomi hugged her mother and kissed her on her weathered cheek. Karen Savoy looked older than her fifty-nine years, but it was understandable. When one worked like she worked, lived where she lived and had to deal with what she had to deal with, you aged fast.

"What you doing here, baby?" she asked softly. "Thought you weren't coming by until tomorrow. Charlie, Tasha, that you?"

"Yes ma'am," Natasha answered. She hugged Naomi's mother right before Charlie did the same.

"I was actually looking for Camille, Mom," Naomi said. She slipped past her mother into the house. As she headed through the living room, towards the hallway that lead to the bedrooms she noticed that everything was spotless - just the way her mother always insisted it was kept.

"Hmm." Karen's lips curled into a frown. "Haven't seen her since she came bustin' in here like a hurricane last night, turned the whole place upside down looking for her passport."

Naomi froze at the door to Camille's old room. Four alarm fire bells went off in her head.

"Her passport?" She asked. She tried to sound calmer than she felt. "What did she want that for?"

"Only the good Lord knows," Miss Savoy ushered Charlie and Natasha inside and closed the door behind them. "She barely spent ten minutes in here. That rotten man-friend of hers waited for her at the gate. He blew his horn the whole time. I swear Camille must be trying to work my last nerve with that one. What she sees in him only the good Lord knows."

"Isn't that what daughters are for?" Charlie asked with a laugh. "To work your last nerve? How are you doing, Miss Savoy? How's things down at Central High?"

"Same as they always been..."

Naomi silently thanked Charlie as she occupied her mother so she could do what she needed to do. She took a deep breath and plunged into Camille's room. Though the rest of the house was immaculate, Camille's room was a mess. The bed was unmade. Dresser drawers were open, the clothes spilled out. Books and loose papers were scattered on the desk and all over the floor. A quick glance in the open closet showed it to be just as torn up. Indeed, hurricane Camille had passed through.

Naomi sorted through the mess for anything that could tell her where the young woman was. At least she knew two things. One, that she had been right to think that Camille's trifling boyfriend was involved and two, the money from Naomi's check had probably gone into a plane ticket. But that made things even more complicated. Where would Camille go the week before Naomi's wedding? Camille was spontaneous but even she wasn't that selfish. Wherever she went, she had planned to be back before the wedding. But why would she spend money for a plane ticket to go away for just a few days? And the fact that she needed her passport meant that she probably left the country. But, for where? Was Andre with her?

Naomi flipped through the papers on the desk and the floor. There was nothing but old study notes and returned test papers. A rifle through her drawers produced a pack of cigarettes and some buds of marijuana but nothing else worth mentioning. She would ream into Camille about the smoking once she laid her hands on her.

Nothing under the bed. Only clothes in the closets. Naomi lifted up the bed sheets and froze. Camille's laptop sat hidden under the covers. She had left it?

Naomi sunk down onto the bed and opened up the laptop.

"Find anything?"

Naomi looked up. Natasha stood in the door.

"Not sure yet." Naomi turned back to the computer and tried different passwords to unlock it. "She left her laptop. I think she wasn't planning on being gone long."

"That could be a good thing right?" Natasha sunk down onto the other side of the bed beside Naomi. "That means she will probably be back soon. Right?"

Naomi wished she could be that optimistic. But she knew her family too well for that.

"If I can get into her computer, I can probably figure this...got it!"

Her fifth attempt worked. Camille had given her her email password once when she needed Naomi to print some documents for her. Naomi was sure she would have changed it. But apparently she hadn't. And apparently she used that one password for everything.

Several internet windows were still open once the

computer was unlocked, including her email. One glance gave Naomi what she wanted.

"Is that a ticket reservation?" Natasha peered over Naomi's shoulder.

"Two tickets," Naomi responded. "For a return flight."

"Where to?"

Naomi squeezed her eyes shut as her head began to pound.

"To Trinidad."

Chapter Five

"Did you call him?"

They were in the parking lot of a McDonalds. Naomi paced, her cell phone squeezed so tightly between her fingers that her palms ached.

"Yes."

"How long will it take for him to call you back?"

"I don't know. A few minutes? A few hours? Days?" Maybe never. Naomi had little confidence that the message she left her brother would be delivered, despite the fact that it had been labelled as urgent. Matter of fact, she wouldn't normally even have attempted contacting him. But this wasn't normal. And given the circumstances he might be one of the only people who knew where Camille was going and why.

"Do you think he really knows where she is?" Natasha had asked.

"I don't know."

"But she did see him recently, didn't she? So he might know..."

Naomi exploded. "I don't know! I don't flippin' know! God, Natasha," Naomi exclaimed. "I am just trying anything I can to figure out what is going on with Camille so could you stop badgering me? It's not helping!"

"Alright, alright," Charlie tried to pacify the situation from where she stood leaning against the side of the car. "She's just concerned that's all. We all are. You're not the only one worried about Camille you know."

Naomi pressed her fingertips against her eyes and let out a deep breath.

"I'm sorry, Natasha, I just...."

"Forget it," Natasha said coldly and folded her arms. "We're all a little on edge right now."

"I know, but I shouldn't have..."

The phone rang.

"Hello?" Naomi answered before she looked at the screen.

"Hey, Red." The deep husky voice flowed over her like velvet. "How's my girl?"

"Jordan, hey."

He wasn't whom she had expected but the sound of his voice calmed her frayed nerves.

"How was your afternoon with the girls?" he asked. He sounded like he was home already. It was only a little after six p.m., but maybe he was still dealing with jet lag from his trip.

"It was...interesting."

He chuckled. "I know what that means. Amanda must have been up to something..."

He continued to talk but Naomi had a hard time paying attention. She didn't want to get the call from her brother while she was on the phone with Jordan. It would bring up too many questions when she had to explain why she needed to go immediately. It would mean she would have to lie to him later, and she couldn't lie. She could omit the truth when she needed to, but she couldn't outright lie. Not to him.

"...Red?"

"Huh?"

"Did you find her?"

"Find who?"

"Camille," Jordan said patiently. "Amanda mentioned that you had to leave the spa early cause something came up with her."

"Oh...uh, no we haven't found her yet," Naomi bit her lip. "Still looking."

"Yeah?" he sounded a touch concerned. "Any leads?"

"Any leads?" Naomi repeated the question as she tried to buy herself time. No way could she tell Jordan that Camille took off to Trinidad even though Natasha silently mouthed, "Tell him the truth."

"Yeah, do you have any clue where she might be?"

Naomi watched Charlie push herself off the side of the car and turn her back to them as she walked away to take a phone call.

"My mother said she came by the house last night, but she didn't tell her where she was going," Naomi said finally.

Natasha rolled her eyes.

"You sound worried."

Naomi sighed. "I am. You know how she is Jordan. She could be anywhere."

"Yeah. But she knows that this weekend is important to you. She'll show up.

Naomi bit her lip. Camille might have good intentions about showing up. But if something happened to her...

"Naomi...is everything okay?"

She snapped to attention. Jordan had used her name. He never called her Naomi unless he was mad or things were serious.

"Honestly, babe, I don't know. I feel really nervous about her being missing like this and I am doing everything I can to find out where she is."

There. That was the most truthful thing she had said during the whole phone call.

"I understand," he said. "Guess I won't be seeing you tonight after all."

"I don't think ...."

There was a beep on the line. Naomi pulled the phone away from her ear to look at the screen. He was calling.

"Babe, I gotta go." She ended the call with Jordan before he could even respond and picked up the incoming call.

"Hello," Naomi said anxiously.

"This is the Hudson County Jail, I have a call for Naomi Savoy. Can you confirm that this is who I am speaking with?"

"This is Naomi Savoy."

"Do you accept the charges for this call?"

"Yes."

"Hold please."

Naomi grabbed Natasha's hand as she listened to the silence on the other end of the line. A few moments later, a gravelly voice came through the line.

"Naomi?"

"Nigel! You called back."

"You said it was urgent."

Naomi hesitated, still shaken by the strangeness of the voice on the other end even though she knew it was her brother. She couldn't remember the last time she had spoken to him. No, that was a lie. She could remember. It was the day he was sentenced in court, right before he went to Rikers. The day he had asked her to take care of his daughter.

"It's about Camille."

"What's wrong with my little girl?"

"She's not so little anymore," Naomi replied. "I think she might be in trouble. She took off to Trinidad, Nigel. Without telling anyone. She went to mom's last night and got her passport. I found her trip itinerary on her computer. She left this morning for Port of Spain."

Nigel let out a slew of curse words.

"How could you let this happen, Nay?"

"Let this happen?" Naomi snapped back. "She is twenty-one years old, not eleven like she was when you got sent away. I can't watch her twenty-four hours a day. She doesn't even tell me anything anyway. I didn't even know she went to see you last week until after the fact."

"That's cause you're too hard on her, Nay," Nigel protested. "She told me how you ride her about school and boyfriends. She says it feels like she has two mothers."

"That's cause our mother is too tired from working and dealing with all your mess to give her the kind of attention she needed," Naomi hissed. "And while she was telling you about the way I ruin her life, did she tell you that I pay for her school too? Give her money to take care of books and food? Put clothes on her ungrateful behind? Make time for her every week? Did she tell you all that too? Did she tell you how I have lied to my fiancé for her? For you?"

"No, you lied to your fiancé for yourself," Nigel said flatly. "Because you think if he knew who you really were, where you really came from, he wouldn't stick around."

The truth stung like a slap to the face, but Naomi didn't have time to linger on it.

"Look, I didn't call to argue with you," She retreated into the safer topic of the situation at hand. "I just needed to know if she said anything to you about this, if you knew what might be going on with her."

She heard her brother sigh. "No, Sis. I don't know anything about her going to Trinidad or why she's doing it. The only thing we talked about while she was here was how she was doing. I was trying to get her to adjust to the idea that I might get deported. She needs to get used to the idea of me not being around...."

"Wait, you're getting deported?" Naomi asked, blindsided by the reality that her brother might be more than a little far away. "But I thought your case was under appeal? I thought that was why they sent you back here to Hudson?"

"Hudson is where they send immigrants before they send them home, Sis. Plus, I don't have the best lawyer so this might be the end of the line for me."

"Why didn't you say something?" Naomi cried. "We could have gotten you a better lawyer. Someone who is good at this stuff."

"No, you all have done enough for me. You've dealt with my expenses, made sure I have money in here, took care of Camille. It's enough. It's time for me to be responsible and take whatever is coming my way," Nigel said. "It's not like I don't deserve it. It's not like I wasn't warned before I made a mess of my life."

Naomi swatted at the tears that escaped down her cheek. "Nige, not this. Not after everything..."

"Don't cry, baby sis," he said gently. "I've made peace with it. It's time. Just take care of my daughter for me. Camille is the best part of me, and I know you only ride her because you want what's best for her. So I'm counting on you to make sure she is okay, and help her make peace with this too."

Naomi tried to keep back her sobs but she couldn't. Her feelings for her brother were complicated on any given day. Resentment for not being there for her before he went in and then after. Anger for what he put her mother through, the long trips she would make to the jail to see him, the money she poured into lawyers for him, the tears she cried at night for him. Sorrow, for Camille having to grow up like Naomi had, without a father. But there was always love. Love like an ocean. Because at the end of the day, he was still her big brother. He was still her hero when it mattered, and she couldn't imagine life with him gone.

"One minute!"

"Look Naomi, I gotta go," Nigel said. "Promise me you will do what you can to find her."

"I will."

"Promise me, Nay," he insisted.

"I promise," Naomi said. "I'll bring her home."

Exhaustion poured over Naomi when the call ended. She didn't realize how far she had walked away from her friends until she turned around and noticed that they were halfway across the parking lot. Their heads were together. They talked intensely. But as soon as Naomi drew near, they stopped.

Naomi looked from Charlie to Natasha. Charlie wore her poker face, but fear was written all over Natasha's. Whatever was going on, Naomi already knew she wouldn't like it.

"Just tell me."

Charlie and Natasha exchanged a look.

Natasha glared at Charlie. "Tell her."

"So I kind of know Andre..."

Naomi frowned. "What do you mean you kind of know him?"

"He's from around here. My cousin used to date his brother. She says they used to..."

Charlie paused and looked over at Natasha who was looking at the ground.

"Spit it out, Charlie," Naomi snapped. "They used to what?"

"They used to sell Molly at parties."

Naomi fell back hard against the car as the world began to swim.

"Tell her the rest," Natasha said.

"Tell her the rest?" Charlie exclaimed as she scowled at Natasha. "Look at her! She's about to pass out from what I just told her."

"Look, we don't have time to play around," Natasha snapped. "If Camille left this morning and is planning to be back in three days then she might already be in serious trouble. Tell her the rest!"

Naomi turned her eyes to Charlie. Her beautiful, olive toned friend stared at her with sympathy.

"Look Naomi, it's probably already too late. There's nothing you can do, just let her go and come back and then..."

"Shut up!" Natasha yelled at Charlie. "Do you even hear yourself?"

Natasha turned to Naomi. "Charlie's cousin said Andre went to Trinidad yesterday morning. He went to pick up a shipment and he probably   took Camille with him too."

"Why would he take her?" Naomi asked. She pushed back against the picture in her mind. "What does she have to do with this?"

"Because he needs someone to bring it back," Charlie said quietly.

"She's his mule," Natasha said. Her eyes watered. She covered her mouth with her hand briefly. "Camille went to swallow pellets, Naomi. She's coming back with a stomach full of cocaine."

Chapter Six

Naomi sat at the kitchen counter in her apartment alone. The lights were off. All except the one above the stove. Its yellow-reddish glow seemed to shine a spotlight on the clear bottle of unopened vodka that sat on the counter in front of her. It was Smirnoff. It used to be her drink of choice, before it stole her life from her. Now, it had no power over her. She had purchased this bottle eight months ago just to make sure.

But tonight, she wasn't sure. Tonight she craved the sensation of the harsh liquid burning a path down her throat. The liquid fire in her stomach. The headiness that came after a few shots. She wanted nothing more.

Except maybe Jordan.

But she couldn't face him. Not tonight. Not with all her secrets exposed. Not while her world fell apart.

She pushed the glass closer to the bottle.

Eight months without a drink. She remembered a time she couldn't go eight days without one. Times she couldn't get out of bed because she was so drunk. No one knew how far down the rabbit hole she had gone. Only Natasha. Natasha was the one who had to hold it down when she couldn't. She laughed out loud when she considered that for four years Jordan thought she didn't drink at all. So many secrets.

She ran her finger down the side of the bottle.

God help her, she wanted that drink.

Her cell phone rang. She didn't even look at her purse. It

sat on the table near the door. Talking to anyone right now was out of the question. She still needed to figure out what she was going to do. How was she going to find Camille? She had nowhere to start.

The cell phone stopped. Then the landline by the refrigerator began. She glanced up at it then back at the bottle. Maybe she should go see Charlie's cousin. Maybe she knew where in Trinidad her niece was.

"Naomi, it's me. Pick up the phone."

The answering machine had kicked in. But even the urgency in Charlie's voice couldn't move her.

"Come on pick up....okay, fine. Just wanted to let you know that I talked to my cousin. She said they're staying somewhere in Port of Spain. Probably with some friends of Andre near Victoria Square. She said Andre's done this before and that Camille will be fine. My cousin said she even did it once. Camille will be back in three days and everything will be...."

Naomi didn't hear the rest as the bottle of vodka smashed into the phone, knocked the handset off the wall sending shards of glass and alcohol all over the kitchen floor. She walked over to the phone without thinking and grabbed the receiver.

"Are you stupid?" she screamed. "My niece is about to swallow God knows how many pellets of cocaine. Cocaine, Charlie! If one bursts in her stomach, she's dead. If they catch her at either airport, she's dead. And even if she doesn't get caught, the dregs of society that she is doing this for could kill her for any reason. So don't call my home and tell me it will be fine. It will NOT be fine."

Naomi slammed the phone against the wall. It was only when she was about to walk away that she realized she stood amid broken glass with splinters all over her feet. The pain registered to her at the same time. She tried to move, but every step was painful. She was stuck - in more ways than one. The thought made her cry. Sobs flowed from her body as she leaned against the refrigerator not sure what to do about anything from the immediate situation of the glass, to the more serious problem of her sister, to the far-reaching issue of her marrying a man who really didn't know her at all.

She didn't know how long she stood there crying. But that was where Jordan found her when he let himself into her apartment with the key she had given him.

"Red, baby, what's going on?" He rushed over to the kitchen where she stood crying. "What happened to your phone...why is there glass...that smell...is that alcohol?"

Naomi began to explain. Everything came out in sobs and moaning. She tried to wipe the tears away but they kept coming.

"Shhh, it's okay honey, I got you." Jordan stepped carefully through the glass in his shoe-clad feet. He slipped his hands around her and under her knees, lifted her out of the mess, and took her out of the kitchen.

Naomi wrapped her arms around his neck. She cried into the collar of his black, Kenneth Cole shirt, not sure why he had come over, but glad he had. It was just like Jordan to show up exactly when she needed him. He always had perfect timing with her. Always.

He laid her gently on the couch and began to move away. She tightened her grip on him, not ready to be away from the comfort of his arms yet.

"I'll be right back." His soothing voice soft against her ear. "I just want to fix those beautiful feet of yours. Can you let me do that, baby?"

She nodded and released him long enough for him to leave the room. He returned with tweezers, a warm cloth and ointment. Jordan sat at one end of the couch. He moved her feet into his lap and patiently removed the splinters, one by one, from her soles. She watched in awe as he touched her feet gently. It wasn't as if she had beautiful feet either. They weren't hideous, but they were rougher in a few spots from too much walking barefoot. But Jordan didn't seem to care. His fingers swept over each part, as he made sure he got all the glass out. Naomi studied his form; the unhurried expression on his face, the way he was at ease with every part of her, her heart ached. She didn't deserve this man. And when he finally figured it out, he would break her heart.

"I have to tell you something."

He placed a dab of ointment on his fingers then began to smooth it across the sole of her foot.

"I'm listening."

She sighed. It was hard to focus as he lightly massaged her feet like that.

"I used to...I was...I am an alcoholic."

His hands paused, but he didn't look up at her. After a moment, he continued his light touch.

She ran a hand nervously through her hair. "Pretty much since college, I've been what they call, a functional drunk. I could drink all night and still show up for class the next morning. I would feel like trash but I could get through the day. I toned it down a lot when I started Street Life. But last year it...it got really bad. For a few weeks, Natasha pretty much had to take over."

He frowned. "Was that around the time we..."

"Yeah." Naomi said. She remembered how destroyed she had been during the two months she and Jordan had broken things off. She had gone days without being sober.

"After that, I realized I needed serious help and I saw someone. I've been completely sober for about eight months now."

He switched feet then began his routine again. Slather with ointment, light massage to her heel, instep, then toes. He seemed to be working through what she just told him.

"What about tonight?" he asked.

"That was just an old bottle," Naomi said. "I've had it for eight months, just to prove to myself that the alcohol had no hold over me. I didn't drink any tonight. I just...threw it against the wall."

"Wanna tell me why?"

Yes.

No.

Naomi sighed.

"Camille hasn't shown up, Jordan," Naomi began. "And I feel...I know that she is in trouble."

"How do you know?"

"She lied to me about doing summer school," Naomi continued, sticking with the safe information. "I went over there and her dorm room was cleaned out. Her RA said she had already checked out for the semester."

"So maybe she decided to commute," he leaned back against the couch. "Or bunk with friends."

"Then why did she cash the check?" Naomi asked. "Where's the money I gave her to pay for the extra weeks on campus?"

He had no answer for that.

Jordan was the youngest of his siblings. The only boy of his parents' three children. He didn't really understand what it was like to be an older sibling. To be responsible for someone younger than him the way Naomi felt responsible for Camille.

"What about your mom?"

Naomi shook her head. "She doesn't know where she is either."

Tears welled up in her eyes again as she thought about what her sister could be doing at that very moment. Camille was in a country she didn't know with a man who was willing to use her body as a transport vehicle for illegal substances. To him, Camille would be as valuable as the street value of the drugs she was able to carry. No doubt, if things went south, he would ditch her and leave her to sort things out on her own. If that was the case, there was no one Camille could call. It wasn't like she had grown up in Port of Spain like Naomi and Nigel had. She had only been there a few times. She barely knew the family they had living there. She would basically be alone.

"I can't stop thinking about what could happen to her." Naomi's voice shook as she tried to hold back the sobs. "What if someone's hurt her? What if she needs help but can't get to anyone? What if she's suffering all alone? What if..."

Jordan moved to Naomi's end of the couch. He gathered her into his arm as her sobs stole her words.

"Shhh. It's okay," he whispered. "It's going to be okay."

She wanted to believe him, but it was hard. She had so little faith in life turning out well anymore.

She heard him sigh before he spoke again. Then he did exactly what she expected him to do.

"Dear Father, we place Camille in your hands. You know where she is. Keep her safe. Bring her home. We ask you because we know You can. Amen."

Naomi's faith was more of a second thought. But Jordan's was a way of life. There was nothing that He didn't pray about - didn't seek God's guidance on. But his way was very practical and to the point. He treated His faith like He did life. Everything was either black or white. It was either truth or a lie. You either believed that God could take care of everything or you didn't believe in Him at all. Your faith was either going to be the center of your life or not a part of it. In his undemanding way, he was always steady. Always sure. He was everything Naomi, with her doubts and second-guessing, was not.

"Thank you for that," she said.

"I know you're almost certain something is wrong," he said against her hair. "But I believe she's going to be alright. No matter what she's gotten herself into, God will keep her safe."

Naomi pulled her legs up under her. She felt safe nestled in Jordan's arms as they sat in silence.

"How many times have we been here like this?" She asked after a long moment. "Curled up in each other's arms, me worrying, you praying?"

He gave a short chuckle. "More than a few."

"Like the day I put my house back on the market," Naomi said. "Or the day you decided to leave the agency and go independent."

"The time after the accident, when I had to have the MRI."

"Oh God," Naomi groaned. "I was really worried for that one."

"Yeah, you were." He rubbed her arm slowly, his mouth curved into a small smile. "You would have thought you were the one having the tests."

"It sure felt like it," Naomi said.

"And of course, the month after we got back together," Jordan continued. "Right before I asked you to marry me."

Naomi smiled for the first time all evening. "I think that time, you were the one worrying, and I was the one praying."

Jordan chuckled. "Yeah. I think you're right. I was so worried I would mess things up again..."

"And I prayed that I wouldn't," Naomi said.

He tipped her chin up to look at him. "I am glad you said yes."

She rested her hand on his cheek, traced the curve of his strong, taut mouth with her thumb. "I'm glad you asked."

She eased him towards her, pressed her lips against his for a moment before opening up and letting him in. This man, he was enough.

"I am sorry I didn't tell you," she whispered against his mouth.

He rested his forehead against hers. "You can always trust me, Red. You know that right?"

She sighed. She wished she could say yes. Wished she could be that sure. Instead, she sealed the question off with a kiss, and left the answer for a time when it would be what they both wanted it to be.

Chapter Seven

"Check in is now open for Flight BW 521 to Port of Spain. Passengers for this flight, if you have not yet done so, please proceed to check-in at terminal four."

Naomi stood at the sound of the announcement and reached for her single piece of carry-on luggage.

"Naomi, this is B.S. and you know it. How can you leave like this without telling Jordan?"

"And what exactly should I say to him, Natasha?" Naomi hoisted her oversized purse onto her shoulder. "Hey baby, I'm going to Trinidad to look for my niece who may or may not be planning to stuff her gut with drugs to smuggle into the country. And oh, by the way, when I say niece, I mean Camille, who is actually not my sister but the daughter of my incarcerated brother whom I never told you about."

"Listen, I told you years ago to tell Jordan about Nigel," Natasha wagged a finger at her friend. "You were the one who was like, oh we're just dating, it doesn't matter..."

"Because back then we were just dating and it didn't matter..."

"And yet here we are, four years later with you engaged and still lying to him about it." Natasha took a deep breath and shook her head. "You cannot possibly think there is any way this is going to end well, Naomi."

Naomi rolled her luggage behind her as she headed to check-in for her flight.

"Natasha, you're making way too big a deal about this," Naomi tried to sound rational. "The way I see it, I'll be in

Port of Spain by midday, sort this crap out in twenty four hours and be back by Thursday night, three whole days before the wedding."

"And how exactly do you plan to find your sister whom you didn't even know was going to Trinidad and has a twenty-four hour head start on you?" Natasha's heels clicked as she walked along behind Naomi. "I know Trinidad is small, but it's still more than 5000 square miles with over a million people. You got some special resources I don't know about?"

Naomi wrinkled her nose but didn't look at her friend. "Maybe."

"Maybe?" Natasha echoed. "Like wha..."

Natasha grabbed Naomi's arm so suddenly, she nearly fell on her behind. But before Naomi could protest, Natasha had whirled her around to face her.

"Naomi, please tell me you didn't...."

Naomi couldn't hold her friend's intense gaze. "I had to..."

"Oh my God..." Natasha seemed to lose her strength as she sat down hard on Naomi's suitcase.

"He's a police officer, a Sergeant," Naomi protested. "He can help me find her..."

"He can lead you off a freakin' cliff," Natasha hissed. She stared incredulously at her friend. "Are you seriously this dense that you would even consider having anything to do with that man again?"

"'Tasha, he's not that bad...."

"Not that bad?" Natasha screeched. "Have you lost your long term memory? Do you remember what happened ten months ago? I almost lost you!"

"That wasn't his   fault...."

"It was completely his fault..."

"But things are different now," Naomi protested.

"They always end up the same when he is around," Natasha argued. "It was like that in college, and it was like that last year when he came to visit."

"But I am different now," Naomi insisted. "I am not that girl anymore."

Natasha shook her head. She dug into her purse. "I can't deal with this. You want to pour your life down the drain again fine, but someone else will have to supervise it."

She pulled out her cell phone and dialed. "I don't have the energy to watch you do that to yourself again. I'm calling Jordan."

"No!" Naomi grabbed Natasha's phone from her fingers. "No. He can't....I can't....not Jordan."

"Why? This is your husband-to-be," Natasha snapped. "He should know about this. Does he even know what happened last year?"

"Yes," Naomi said, finally able to win some points back with her friend. "I told him last night. About the alcohol, about how bad it got."

"Finally," Natasha said, only slightly relieved. "Did you tell him about the alcohol poisoning?"

Naomi closed her eyes and shuddered as the memory washed over her. "I told him it was bad and that I got treatment."

Natasha stood up and touched her friend's arm. "Then Nay-Nay, why stop there? Why not tell him everything? This is your window to come clean, your opportunity to put it all out there and let him prove that he is the man we know he is, that he is going to love you no matter what."

Naomi was tempted. Oh boy was she tempted. And that

temptation had never been stronger than last night. She had sat on her couch in Jordan's arms and talked to him until two in the morning. They talked like they used to back when they first got together. Before they fell into the routine of being together, before their careers, their lives and even their wedding plans made them forget how much they enjoyed just being with each other.

It had felt like the night when they first met. They had slipped out of the barbeque and took a three-hour walk around the neighborhood while they talked about anything and everything. Last night had been like that.

Despite all that, Naomi had not told him. And even an hour after he left, as she purchased her ticket online and packed her suitcase for Port of Spain, still she had kept him in the dark. Why? Because Nigel was right. She was afraid to lose him. And she would lose him. Maybe they could wink at the alcohol abuse, but there was no way his family would allow him to marry someone with a brother in prison, a niece attempting to smuggle drugs and all the other baggage that came with the Naomi Savoy package. Not with all the political aspirations they had for him; aspirations that Jordan said he didn't want now, but might want later. Her cloudy past would make that impossible for him and their end would be inevitable. And she wasn't sure she could handle the stress of finding her niece while dealing with the stress of having lost the man she loved.

Naomi looked away from Natasha and shrugged. "I don't want to tell him like this. Not with so many things hanging in the balance. I'll do it before the wedding, when I come back."

"I won't lie for you," Natasha warned.

Naomi nodded. "I know."

Naomi slipped her purse off her shoulder and rested it on top of her suitcase.

"Hug me, tell me you love me and wish me luck."

Natasha rolled her eyes, as she put her arms around her friend.

"God, why did you give me this crazy stubborn woman for a best friend?" She murmured as she held her. "Please keep her safe, keep Camille safe, and help them to find each other before either of them gets irreparably hurt. And please help Naomi to trust You, trust that if she is honest with the man You gave her, that You will not allow her heart to be broken. We thank You. Amen."

"Thanks," Naomi said, as she held on to her friend. "I love you too."

"Yeah, whatever," Natasha said letting go. "Get out of here before I change my mind about calling Jordan."

Naomi blew kisses at her best friend before she rushed through airport departures to find her gate. In five hours, she would be back in the place she had once called home. The place where she had spent every summer and a few Christmases until she turned eighteen. The place where memories and regrets lurked around every corner. She really hoped everyone's prayers worked. If there was ever a time she needed God, it was now.

Chapter Eight

"You got the back?"

"I got it."

"Okay let's lift on three....one, two, three!"

Jordan's muscles barely whined as he hoisted his end of the sofa off the driveway in front of his house. His cousin, Malcolm, however wasn't faring as well on his end.

"What in the world....kind....of couch...is this?" Malcolm grunted out as they carried the large tan overstuffed seating unit through the main double doors of the house.

"La-Z-Boy," Jordan said as he backed down the hallway and into what was going to be the den. "As soon as Red and I saw this one, we agreed on it. It's going to be perfect for the den."

"With seven pieces it better be." Malcolm let out a deep breath as he straightened up.

Jordan grinned. "It will be great. When the family comes over, everyone can hang out in here."

"The guys can watch football while the kids play on the carpet." Jordan motioned to the covered area in front of the sofa. "And the ladies will have a view of everything from the kitchen behind."

Malcolm nodded in agreement. "It will be nice having everyone here. And having those sliding doors to the backyard means you can have people out there and have them be a part of things too."

"Exactly." Jordan planted his hands on his hips, looked

out through the huge picture windows as if he were imagining it. "It's going to be great. I can't wait to move in here with Red."

Malcolm grinned. "I'm sure that's not all you can't wait for. I saw that King size bed upstairs. Four years is a long time to hold out."

Jordan slipped his hands into his pockets and shrugged. "It's a conscious decision me and Red made at the beginning. Marriage is hard enough as it is. We wanted to make sure that we could date and evaluate each other with a clear head, without bedroom drama interfering with things."

"But come on man," Malcolm squinted at Jordan. "This is your boy you're talking to. You can't tell me you didn't slip up and hit it even once."

Jordan shot him a look.

"Alright, alright. Backing away from that topic," Malcolm snickered. "I gotta say though, I am real glad you didn't ask me to help you move that bed upstairs."

Jordan chuckled. "Nah. I left that to the professionals. Some jobs are worth the money."

"So this means you're all set for the big day?" Malcolm followed Jordan back out to the front where the remaining four pieces of the sofa sat. They were small, so the men grabbed one each.

"As ready as I can be. Rings are purchased and in hand, tux is ready, hotel booking for the night is taken care of and our flight Monday morning to the honeymoon is booked."

"You tell her where it is yet?"

"Not even a hint," Jordan said with a grin. "Got her packing everything from ski suits to bikinis."

Both men laughed.

"Man, I still can't believe you're marrying her. Well, I

can believe it cause...I've seen her and..." Malcolm let out a low whistle. "Megan Good's got nothing on that chick. But still, with everything going on with her."

"You mean the whole situation with her brother?"

"Yes!" Malcolm set down the couch. "If your parents knew - scratch that. If your momma knew about that, she would have flipped out."

"Yeah, thanks for keeping that between us."

"Like I said, you're my boy." They headed back outside for the last pieces. "Does she even know that you know?"

"Nope."

"She still hasn't told you?"

Jordan let out a deep breath as he grabbed the last piece of the couch. "Nope. But she will."

"When? After the wedding? She should have come out with that a long time ago."

Jordan grimaced. His cousin was right. Naomi should have told him about her brother in prison. In fact, there was a moment the night before, under the soft evening glow as they sat on her couch that he was sure she was going to tell him. After all, she had told him all about her drinking, and he hadn't even known about that. But she still hadn't said a word about her brother. He wondered if there were other things his wife-to-be wasn't sharing with him.

"It's not that easy for her," Jordan said. "Can you imagine what it's like marrying into this family? I still remember the first time Red met mom. This confident, articulate woman that I had fallen in love with turned into a bundle of nerves right before my eyes."

"Well, Lady Lennox is a scary woman," Malcolm conceded. He dropped down onto the piece of furniture he had just brought in. "She even scares me a little, and I've known her all my life. I'll take Uncle G any day of the week."

"Yeah," Jordan walked over to the fridge and grabbed two sodas. "Dad's a pretty cool guy. He loves Red too. Heck, some days I think he likes her more than me."

"Hey, if I had to choose between her face and your ugly mug, I'd choose hers too." Malcolm laughed and grabbed the soda Jordan tossed at him before it smacked him in the face.

"I was hoping you could have your girl look into something for me though," Jordan sat down across from his cousin.

"Which girl?" Malcolm asked with a grin. "I got a lot of different girls doing a lot of different things for me."

"The girl you got to run the background check on Red that I didn't ask for," Jordan said pointedly.

"Hey, you asked if I knew her!"

"Yeah, as in, if you knew her personally," Jordan said. "That wasn't an invitation to have her investigated."

"The way you were sweating the girl before you even talked to her made me know that I needed to run a check," Malcolm said. "You were already too blind to see."

Jordan shook his head, but he remembered clearly the first time he saw Naomi. It had been at the Thirty Under Thirty Awards Gala for young entrepreneurs. She had been in an orange gown that made her skin glow like the sunset. She had caught his eye the moment she walked into the room. But when she went up to speak as part of the reflection of past honorees, she stole his attention. Jordan had known then that he had to meet her. So he waited, and then pulled every favor he had with his sister to get her to invite Naomi to the smaller barbeque event held for the Thirty Under Thirty Board. The night they met for the first time, they had talked for hours. It was still one of the best nights of his life. And he found that most of the best moments in his life now involved Naomi.

He couldn't let her go.

Yes, there were things in her past. But nothing that they couldn't get past. In fact, the most concerning thing was that she had chosen not to tell him about that part of her life. And he had waited for it. Through the two years they casually dated on and off, and then the year after that when they decided to become serious about things. Even after the break-up and during the emotional make-up where she had shared things with him he knew she had never told anyone else. After the engagement, and right up to the moment he walked out of her apartment in the wee hours of the morning, the night before, Naomi still hadn't said a word.

That bothered him.

He had prayed about it. Asked God what direction to take with her. But all he had gotten was the command to wait, and be patient. But how long was he supposed to wait?

"Sometimes I wonder if you are still too blind to see her objectively," Malcolm said. He watched his cousin with concern.

Jordan took a swig from his soda. "I hear what you're saying, cuz. But with Red, it's different."

"Different as in the whole honesty thing is not important?"

"Different as in I know she loves me. I know she's not trying to be dishonest, she's just..." Jordan searched for the right words to explain the woman he loved. "I've spent so much time praying on this, meditating on this....I know that it's supposed to be me and her."

Malcolm raised an eyebrow. "You're that sure?"

Jordan shrugged. "I'm that sure." He chuckled. "Why do

you think that after two months of calling it quits we still ended up back with each other?"

"Cause y'all are both crazy?"

Jordan smiled. "Maybe. But I believe God has a plan. And He's going to work things out with this somehow. It might be messy, but it's going to get worked out."

Malcolm saluted him. "Love your confidence, bruh. What you need my friend for then?"

"I think something may have happened with her sister, Camille." Jordan's brow furrowed as he thought about how distressed Naomi had been the night before. "She's gone missing. Can you get your friend to do a quick search and see if anything turns up?"

Malcolm nodded. "Sure. I'll call her today."

"Great." Jordan stood up and tossed his cousin the keys. "And can you lock up for me when you leave?"

"Wait, where you going?"

"To check some of my other contacts," Jordan headed towards the front door. "Whatever is going on with Camille, I want it sorted out soon. Nothing is stopping this wedding. Absolutely nothing."

Chapter Nine

Summer seemed to have set-up permanent camp in Port of Spain. The heat and humidity hit Naomi like a hot damp towel as she stepped out of the safety of the air conditioned airport into the bright Caribbean sunlight. She was thankful that at least the cool coastal breezes provided moments of relief.

Though she had sunglasses on, she still shaded her eyes as she stood in the taxi bay looking out. Through the sea of brown faces she searched for the one that might be a little familiar. Truth be told, it had been so long since she had seen Latoya that she couldn't be sure she would even recognize her cousin.

"Naomi!"

No need. Her cousin had recognized her.

Naomi turned around at the sound of the voice and saw a slim, dark skinned woman with a not so slim mid-region, running towards her.

"Latoya? Oh my God!"

The two women embraced each other, as much as was possible with half a person between them.

"You're pregnant!" Naomi squealed as she held her cousin back to look at her. "You didn't tell me!"

"I know," Latoya said, a huge smile exposed straight white teeth. "I wanted to surprise you!"

"Well, you did!" Naomi stared at her cousin again. She tried to soak up the change that had happened in the nine years since they had last seen each other. Latoya had barely been twenty when she married her long-time boyfriend, Neil. Now, she was popping out babies. The world had certainly moved along.

She smiled and pulled Latoya into a hug again. "I am so glad to see you."

"Likewise."

"So," Naomi let go of her cousin so she could lead her to the car. "Tell me everything that's been happening."

They caught up on life as the taxi flew through the streets of downtown Port of Spain and into the hills just above the city where Latoya lived. By the time Naomi got to her cousin's home, she had gotten halfway through her part of the catching up.

"So, you and that gorgeous man in all your Facebook pictures are finally getting married," Latoya's flip flops slapped against the marble floor as she headed to the kitchen.

"Yes we are," Naomi grinned as the image of her man's face popped into her mind. "The wedding's Sunday."

Latoya opened the fridge door. "You mean on the seventeenth?"

"No," Naomi leaned against the counter. "The tenth."

Latoya's head popped around the side of the fridge door, a confused expression on her face. "This Sunday? Girl, what the heck are you doing here?"

Naomi sighed and walked away from the counter. She slid into a chair at the breakfast nook.

"Short answer? Camille."

Latoya pursed her lips as she placed a pitcher of juice on the counter. "And the long answer?"

"Girl, you're gonna need to bring that pitcher and two

glasses over here for that."

Once they both sat, Naomi spared no details and told her cousin everything that had transpired in the last few days.

"Nay..." Latoya rubbed both hands over her face tiredly. "I don't even know where to start."

"Just don't start like Natasha did with all the you-need-to-tell-Jordan stuff..."

"Well, you do need to tell Jordan," Latoya said. "But I know you won't. You've always had issues when it came to men."

Naomi's mouth fell open. "What?"

"I don't have time to touch that right now," Latoya waved away the shocked expression on her cousin's face. "My real concern is, how do you plan to locate our little drug dealer now? You know your foreign behind can't be walking around Port of Spain, inquiring about a missing American girl. That's just asking for trouble."

"Garth."

Latoya's raised eyebrow was enough to make Naomi look away.

"Wow, you really are doing everything to ruin things with Jordan, aren't you?"

"What choice do I have?" Naomi asked. "He's the only person I know that would probably be able to find her in the two days I have to get this done."

Latoya wrinkled her nose. "Well, he sure deals with enough dirt to know where to find the scum that have Camille."

Naomi sighed. "The quicker I can deal with this, the quicker I can find Camille and get back home."

"Alright." Latoya took a deep breath then hoisted

herself out of her seat. "Let's go then. Clock's a ticking."

"Wait," Naomi eyed her cousin warily. "You're not coming with us."

"Of course not," Latoya said with a scowl. "Neil would kill me. But you will need a ride to the station. Besides, it's been a while since I've given Garth a piece of my mind. Today feels like the day."

Naomi rolled her eyes but followed her cousin to the door. She didn't know why everyone was getting worked up. Garth was in her past, and she would only be here for two days. What could possibly happen?

Chapter Ten

His precinct was in the heart of Port of Spain and it took a lot off maneuvering through transit buses, honking taxis and pedestrians to get there. Latoya parked her Toyota Rav 4 right in front of the main entrance and shut off the engine. Almost immediately, two men in uniform walked towards her. But as soon as the car door opened and her stomach came into view, they both stopped. Latoya smiled at them and they nodded before going back to their post.

Naomi shook her head. "Amazing."

"Perks of being pregnant."

The distance from the car to the front doors was short but Naomi could feel eyes on her. She pushed her sunglasses a little further up on her nose and held her head straight as she followed her cousin through the doors into the precinct. She was a foreigner. Despite the fact that she had been born in this country, she had been away too long to be considered one of their own. They knew it. It oozed off her skin like an odor, echoed in the American lilt in her speech. There was nothing she could do to hide it. And that's why she needed Latoya. Needed Garth. Without them, she would spend the next two days spinning her wheels.

"Ladies, can I help you?"

The desk officer's question was directed to Latoya, but his eyes were fixed on Naomi. He openly assessed her, wondered what trouble she might cause him on this particular day.

Latoya scowled at the officer. "Yes, I'm looking for Officer Duhaney."

"That's Sergeant Duhaney to you."

His voice was rough. It hit Naomi like the bark of a tree against her bare back. When she turned to look at him, she found that he looked just as wild, the uniform and all it represented did nothing to tame him. Dark eyes, the color of coffee, stood out against nutmeg toned skin. Naomi had thought that officers were required to be clean shaven, but with the deep shadow on his square jawline, Naomi saw that Garth still broke the rules. But the scruffiness didn't take away from him at all. He was still as handsome as she remembered. That never changed.

"Garth, wow, a uniform," Latoya said dryly. "Never seen you in one of those before. Does it help you remember that you're a cop?"

"Nice to see you too, Toya." His tone was dismissive, partly because there was no love lost between the two of them, but mostly because he was too busy staring Naomi down. And as she stared right back without flinching, Naomi suddenly knew exactly why Natasha and Latoya were concerned. Truthfully, they had every right to be.

Waves of hot and cold rushed over her. Her mouth felt dry. Naomi was sure that at any moment she would start shaking.

This was bad.

She remained rooted in place as he slowly strolled over. Garth closed the distance between them until he was so close, she had to look up at him. Naomi could count the tiny hairs on his week old stubble if she had the time and was so inclined.

"I knew you would come back."

She took a deep breath and reminded herself that Camille needed her. That she walked through this valley of death for her. Right now, Camille was all that mattered.

"Can we talk?" Naomi asked.

Garth's lips slowly spread into a smile that made Naomi's gut tighten. "Sure, sweetheart. We can talk anytime you want."

"Maybe somewhere less...crowded," Naomi glanced around.

He nodded and the two women followed him through the precinct, down a hall and into a small office. Garth sat in the battered office chair on one side of the dinosaur of a desk while Naomi and Latoya took the two hard plastic chairs on the other side of it. An overhead fan spun lazily above them. It did nothing to cool the room or help with the sweat that trickled down Naomi's spine.

"Camille's missing," Latoya said, getting right to the point. Naomi could tell the woman wanted to be in and out of Garth's presence as soon as possible. "She came here with her boyfriend but he's involved in some kind of drug run to New York."

Garth's face grew steely as he listened to Latoya. He turned his eyes to Naomi.

"When did this happen?"

"Yesterday, as far as I know," Naomi answered. "She didn't tell me she was coming here, but I found her itinerary on her computer. We heard through the grapevine the reason for their visit but have no idea where they might be."

Garth pulled out a pen and a small notepad. "What's this guy's name?"

"Andre. His last name is Whittaker, I think," Naomi answered. "He might be staying with some friends near Victoria Square."

Garth nodded. "I know some people in that area. I'll pass through there and see what I can find out. Anything else you can tell me?"

Naomi opened her purse and pulled out a picture of Camille. She slid it across the table. "I know it's been a while. This is what she looks like now."

As she glanced at the picture of her smiling niece, Naomi blinked back tears. When she spoke her voice came out shaky. "I don't know why she's doing this. Maybe it has to do with Nigel. Maybe it has to do with money. She just always does these things and doesn't think about the consequences. She probably thought she could be in and out in a couple days without me knowing."

"Anyway, we need to find her by tomorrow, before Naomi has to leave and before Camille tries to board a plane with a stomach full of drugs," Latoya said.

Garth frowned at her. "You expect me to figure this out in twenty-four hours? How do you even know she's leaving tomorrow anyway?"

"Because that's what her ticket said," Naomi answered, before Latoya could open her mouth. She shot her a cousin a look that told her to shut up. But it went right over her head.

"And because Naomi is getting married this weekend and Camille would never miss that," Latoya said with smirk. She seemed to enjoy the way Garth's cocky look slid right off his face.

His eyes locked on Naomi's. She tried to look away, but she couldn't.

"You're getting married?"

The guilt settled somewhere in her throat. It choked back her words, so she just nodded. His eyes pierced through her as waves of emotions swept across his face.

"Latoya, could you give us a minute?"

"No."

Both Naomi and Garth looked over at her. She glared back at Garth without flinching.

"Listen, Garth Duhaney, I know you," she narrowed her eyes. "I've known you since you wore knee shorts and we both went to the same elementary school. You were no good then and you're no good now. And if you think I'm gonna let you mess up my cousin's life again, you have another thing coming. Don't let the belly fool you, I will still kick your a-"

"Latoya!"

Naomi placed a hand on her cousin's arm. It was enough to stop her verbal assault, but not enough to cool the fire in her eyes as she glared at Garth. For his part, Garth breathed hard. His jaw locked and his eyes were steely as he glared back at her. Naomi was very glad that the large heavy desk between them stopped the World War Three that was about to happen.

"Look, Garth, all I care about right now is Camille. I have to find her. Will you help us?"

He turned his gaze slowly towards Naomi, his features softened as he did. "I'll do my best. In the meantime, go home and sit tight. I'll give you a call in a few hours and let you know what I find."

Naomi stood. She helped Latoya up with her.

"Thank you," she said. Then she beat a hasty exit out of the office and the precinct before hell on earth broke loose. She said a prayer in her heart. She would need God in more ways than one if any of them planned to make it through the next twenty-four hours.

Chapter Eleven

"So you're really doing this. You're really going to leave this house at eleven at night with that man?"

When Naomi returned from the police station, she had stalked all of Camille's social media platforms to see if she had posted anything since the last time Naomi saw her. There was nothing. And the anxiety of the day combined with her lack of sleep caused her to pass out in Latoya's guest room not long after. She had only been roused several hours later when Garth called, saying he had a lead.

And now here she was. Naomi sat on the steps of the front porch and pulled on her shoes as she listened to Latoya frown behind her from the front door.

"If he ends up finding Camille in this place, I need to be there."

Latoya snorted even as the black SUV pulled up to the end of the driveway. "I hope that's the only thing you find."

Naomi threw her a weary look then stepped into the darkness as she made her way down to Garth's waiting vehicle. Her skin, flushed from nervousness, was cooled by the night air. As Naomi drew closer, the tinted passenger window of the vehicle rolled down.

"Get in," Garth said somewhat impatiently from the still-running vehicle. "We gotta go."

Naomi barely had both feet in the vehicle when it pulled away from the curb. The wheels spun. She threw a look at Garth as she pulled her seatbelt on.

"In a bit of a hurry?" she asked dryly.

"Some of my guys are already on the way to the location," he said gruffly. "I don't want them waiting on me."

Naomi didn't think that was it. But she didn't say anything. In fact, they barely said anything to each other as the vehicle cut through the almost-midnight darkness. Thanks to Garth's break-neck driving, they made it out of the hills and into the city in record time. As they drove past Queen's Park Savannah and then the city's General Hospital, Naomi was pretty certain they were on their way to Victoria Square.

He stopped the vehicle at the corner of Victoria Square and Duke Street then shut off the engine. Naomi reached for the door. She realized that it was locked around the same time she realized that Garth wasn't moving. She couldn't read much from the steely profile he gave her but she knew enough to know that she had been right the first time. It wasn't just about people waiting for him. There was more than that on his mind.

"Were you going to tell me you were getting married?" His voice carried the same coarseness from when he picked her up. He was mad enough that he didn't even look at her.

Naomi considered lying for a moment then changed her mind. "No."

Fiery dark roast eyes whipped around to glare at her. "Why not?"

"Because honestly, Garth, it's none of your business," Naomi said with a shrug.

"But it's my business when you need to find Nigel's kid, right?"

"No, it isn't," Naomi said. "But I asked you to make it your business because you're the only one I know who can help me with this."

Garth gritted his teeth. He swore and slammed his fist against the armrest. Naomi stared out the windshield and let him have his temper tantrum. This was just like Garth. She had known he would react this way sooner or later, and was just glad they could get it out of the way and get on to the business of finding Camille.

"After all we've been through Nay, you should have told me," he growled. "I'm not just some man you shacked up with one time. I was..."

"Yes, that's it, Garth. You were. We were. It's the past, we aren't anything anymore," Naomi interrupted him. "You know that."

He shook his head. "I thought we were at least friends."

"We can't be friends. Even when we were friends, it was poison. We're bad for each other, Garth. And it's better for the both of us if we just keep things as disconnected as they have been for the past year."

She let out a deep breath, glad that she had been finally able to say the words that she should have said years ago. Words that would have saved her a ton of heartache if she had just believed them a lot sooner.

"So it's like that, huh?"

Naomi rubbed her eyes. "Garth, I will always care about you. You know that. We grew up together and I'll never forget that. But we both live different lives now. So let's just let what was, remain what was."

He rubbed a hand over his face and stared out his window a long time.

"Alright." When he finally turned to look at her, he was back to his old over-confident self. "I hear you, Miss Savoy."

Before either of them could say anything more, there was a knock on the window. Garth rolled it down and spoke quietly to someone she couldn't see then rolled it back up.

"Alright, here's what's going to happen. You see that bar over there?"

Naomi nodded as Garth pointed down the street to a spot with the brightest lights on the otherwise subdued street.

"Is that where she is?" Naomi sat forward, but a hand on her arm pressed her back.

"Easy, sweetheart," Garth eased her back. "She might be in there, she might be in the apartment above it, or she might not be there at all. We're just following a lead. And I need you to be calm and promise me that you will follow my lead."

"I will," Naomi reached for the door. Garth's hand slowed her down again.

"I'm serious, Nay." The intensity in his eyes made her pause. "The guys who hang out at this place are not people you want to play with. If they even smell anything suspicious they won't hesitate to shoot. So just stay close and follow me. Got it?"

Tension filled her chest as she realized how serious Garth was. She nodded. "Okay."

The automatic locks for the doors clicked open. They both got out. Naomi fell in step close to Garth as they walked towards the bar. The street was quiet save for the faint sounds of calypso she assumed came from the bar. She rubbed her bare arms in defense against the cool air and glanced around her nervously. She stiffened when she saw a figure walking a few paces behind them.

"Don't worry, he's with us," Garth said quietly.

They were almost at the bar now and already Naomi's eyes were peeled for any sign of her niece. She was so intent that when Garth put his arm around her shoulders and pulled her snug against his side she almost jumped out of her skin.

"What are you..."

"Remember, just go with it," he whispered, his mouth pressed against her ear. His breath felt warm against her neck and her body responded exactly how she wished it wouldn't. She wanted to pull away from him, for her own safety. But they were now at the entrance of the bar and any such movement would attract unwelcomed attention. So Naomi did exactly what he told her to do, she went with it.

She slipped her arm around his waist. They walked in together and took a seat near a corner at the front. It was a good spot. They could see most of the room and there was no one behind them. Naomi flashed a smile at Garth as her eyes discreetly perused the room. He raised an eyebrow at her questioningly. She shook her head slightly. Thus far, no sign of Camille.

The room, however, was filled with an assortment of characters. Most of the seats at the bar were taken and there were scatterings of people in groups of twos and threes at the small tables in the middle. Music blared from the speakers stacked up to the ceiling in a corner. Couples packed together tightly, danced closely under the dim lights of the open area at the back. She didn't have a great view of the booths down the side but the one in the opposite corner of the bar had a large noisy group of mostly men.

Garth slipped his arm around the back of her chair then leaned close to her ear again.

"I'm gonna get us some drinks at the bar and figure out what's going on."

"Okay."

Then before she knew what had happened, Garth

dropped a quick kiss on her lips and walked away.

Naomi sat in her seat, stunned. She had wondered before if Garth was taking advantage of this situation, the way his arm fell possessively around her shoulders, the way his hand slid down and grazed her behind as he seated her. Now, she knew he was. He had her in a tight spot. But if he thought he was going to use it to get his way, he had another thing coming.

Naomi glanced around the room again as she waited, this time she looked for Andre. She saw no sign of him. She started to doubt Garth's intel. At just that moment, he returned with two glasses of beer.

"I thought we were working," Naomi said as he slid both glasses onto the table.

"We're in a bar, Nay," he said dryly. "What did you think I was gonna order, ginger ale?"

"Well, you should have," Naomi curled her lips. "Cause I don't drink. And by the way, you try anything like what you just pulled again and you'll be sorry."

He grinned. "Come on, Naomi. I can't believe a big girl like you got scared after just one kiss. We've done a lot more than that in the past."

"How about you focus on remembering that last part - in the past?"

"Listen, we're undercover," he said as he slipped his arm around her chair again and leaned in. "We gotta do what we have to do to maintain the image. Now drink your beer or I'll be forced to kiss you again."

Naomi ran a finger down his chest. She felt the hard muscles beneath, and leaned close to his ear. "You kiss me again, and I'll pour this drink down your pants."

He laughed heartily. "Glad to see some things haven't

changed."

"Did you find out anything from the bartender?" Naomi asked.

"Only that Andre was here last night and passed by earlier today," Garth took a swig of his beer. "The owner of the bar lives upstairs and is a friend of his but he's not here tonight. He might come back later though. He doesn't exactly have a schedule."

"What about Camille? Has he seen her?"

"Didn't ask," Garth said. "I don't want word getting around that we're looking for her. It might get back to Andre and then we may never be able to find him."

Naomi stood up suddenly. The move elicited a look of surprise from Garth.

"Where are you going?"

"To the ladies room."

He looked like he wanted to argue with her but she didn't give him a chance. If she did, he might figure out what her actual plan was. She strode easily across the busy room and down the side past the booths she previously couldn't see. There were some interesting activities going on in a couple of them, but no Andre and no Camille.

She pushed the door with the female symbol on it and found herself in an aging two stall bathroom with dingy tiles and peeling walls. Both stalls were empty. Naomi waited a few moments before heading back to the exit.

She sidled out the door into the hallway. Instead of heading back to the table, she glanced both ways then slipped quietly out the back door at the end of the hallway into the darkness of the night. The cool air brought a welcome contrast to the hot sticky atmosphere inside the bar. Naomi leaned against the back of the building and looked around the small paved courtyard area. It was mostly dark, lit only by the moon and the light that streamed down below from an upstairs window. On one side and along the back, a high concrete wall separated the courtyard from the neighbors' property. To her right, however, a staircase on the side of the L shaped building led to what could be the apartment upstairs. Naomi's heart pounded faster as she looked up at the single window. A sheer curtain muted the light. Naomi couldn't tell what was going on behind it, but didn't see any movement either. She looked back at the door that led to the bar then back at the stairs. The evening air shook the wide leaves of a banana tree that grew close to the back wall and pushed against her, as if warning her to go back. But she couldn't. Her heart beat like a bass drum. Her limbs shook, but she had to do it. Naomi had to see if Camille was in that room. What if something had gone wrong and they had left her up there to die? What if this was the only chance she had to save her. She couldn't pass that up.

With another glance around the courtyard, she scurried over to the stairs, made the first step, then took the rest two at a time. Halfway up she thought she heard something. She froze. Her eyes peeled around the courtyard for any sign of movement. There was scratching again, and then a stray cat crawled out from the shadows into the open. Naomi let out the breath she held, as the cat crossed the yard, then disappeared through a hole in the back wall.

She gritted her teeth. This was taking too long. Garth would look for her soon. It was only when she got to the top of the stairs that it occurred to her that the door might be locked.

"God, please don't let it be locked, and please let Camille be in there and safe."

She held her breath as she tried the handle of the door. It gave easily beneath her fingers. With a little push it swung open. From her position at the door, the room looked empty. She could see a couch and the blue lights that reflected off the wall told her a TV was on. Naomi stuck her head inside and confirmed that she was right.

It was a small space, but it was littered with an assortment of things. Soda cans and beer bottles sat on the table. Old newspaper was strewn haphazardly on the floor. One discarded sneaker here, a couple of flip flops there. A pair of new Timberlands, probably size six.

Naomi froze.

Those were Camille's Timberlands. She was almost sure. She walked over, picked them up and looked the boots over. Sure enough, Camille's initials were marked discreetly on the inside, where she marked all her shoes so her roommate wouldn't take off with them and claim they were hers.

Energy surged through Naomi as she realized her niece was there, or had been very recently.

"Camille!"

She tore through the room. Naomi opened the first door she saw to her right. It was a bathroom. Empty. But the bucket on the floor with two white packets, the shape of size D-batteries, was what made cold sweat break out across her body.

"Camille!"

She shoved open the next door and found herself in an unlit room. The light from the living room streamed in. It revealed part of a bed. Naomi felt the wall at the side of the door. Her fingers hit a switch. She flicked it up and down but nothing happened. As her eyes adjusted to the darkness, she saw a figure on the bed, unmoving. She crept over, stumbled over a bag on the ground and almost fell on the bed herself.

"Camille?" she called out softly, almost afraid to get an

answer. Her shoe kicked something else. The leg of a lamp. She felt the base until her fingers found the nob. Light flooded the room. A moment later, dread flooded Naomi's heart.

"Camille!" She shook the still body of her niece, even as tears began to fall down her cheeks. "Camille, wake up. Please!"

She slapped the young woman's face a few times. Camille stirred; a groan escaped her lips.

"Oh thank God!" Naomi breathed. "Camille, you have to get up. We have to go."

Camille groaned some more and then she clutched her stomach. When she finally opened her eyes, they were watery and bloodshot. She tried to lift her head but couldn't seem to find the energy.

"Naomi?"

"Yes, hunny. It's me."

Camille started crying, rivers of tears rolled down her cheeks. Naomi couldn't stop her own tears as she looked at her niece. She looked worse than she had ever seen her. But there was no time for this. Right now, they needed to get out of there.

"We gotta get out of here, hun." Naomi slipped her arm under Camille's and managed to get her in an upright position. "I need you to help me though, Cam. I can't carry you."

Still the tears flowed, but Camille nodded and pushed her feet down to the ground. Naomi helped her untangle the sheets from her legs.

"Come on, let's go," Naomi pulled her to her feet.

"I can't...." Camille moaned, her weight pulled Naomi down.

"Yes, you can," Naomi hissed. "And you will."

Naomi didn't know if Camille agreed, but she sniffled and tried to hold herself up again. They were halfway to the bedroom door when they heard a door slam and the sound of footsteps. Panic sliced through Naomi. Camille started crying again. She let go and crumpled to the floor at Naomi's feet.

"Camille!" Naomi hissed, she turned towards her niece, but the fear in her eyes made her stop.

Naomi turned around. Angry eyes stared at her. Then before she uttered a word, the world went black.

Chapter Twelve

This was one of the reasons Naomi had stopped drinking. The hangovers. It felt like someone had cracked her skull open and knocked a bowling ball around inside. Except she hadn't been drinking so this couldn't be a hangover. So why was there pain with every movement? Why was she moving?

Naomi tried to remember what had happened but her head hurt too much and the world felt topsy-turvy. She cracked open her eyes and realized why.

"Let me go!" With the little energy she had, she yelled and beat on the back of the man who carried her fireman style over his shoulder. At least she thought it was a man. She was almost 140lbs. She didn't know many women who could handle all that.

Despite her protests however, her captor continued carrying her. He increased his pace. A wave of nausea washed over her. Naomi took a deep breath. Then before it came again, she dug her nails into the back of the man who carried her. She was about to attempt a bite next when she felt herself flipped over suddenly and propelled backwards.

She screamed as she tumbled backwards and made a rough landing on her feet.

"What is wrong with you?"

She blinked. "Garth?"

"Who else?" he asked gruffly. His hand gripped her upper arm as he hurried her down the street. Before she could say another word, he opened the door of the SUV and hustled her inside. Naomi closed her eyes and rubbed her aching head. She still felt a bit nauseous.

"What's going on?" she asked weakly. "What happened?"

"You almost got yourself killed, that's what," Garth said dryly as he floored the gas pedal and took off down the road, away from the still open bar. "Do you know how stupid it was going upstairs into that room like that? Those guys could have shot you in the face, raped you, and tossed you into the harbour. What the hell were you thinking, Naomi?"

The evening's events suddenly rushed back to Naomi and she groaned. "Camille. Where's Camille? Did you get her?"

"No."

"No?" Naomi cried, alarm all over her features. She grabbed at Garth's arm. "You have to go back. I can't leave her there. She's gonna die..."

He pulled his arm away. "I don't have to do anything," he snapped. "Besides, she's not even there anymore. That guy that gun butted you wanted to kill you. Our inside man had to convince him to take Camille and let him take care of you. They'll keep her alive. Camille already has the pellets in her. They're not going to take a risk on their $50,000."

Naomi was too shocked to respond. All she could see was Camille's face, her bloodshot eyes, her lifeless body before she managed to wake her up. What if next time she couldn't wake her? And now Garth was telling her Camille already had all those narcotics inside her...

Naomi put her head between her legs and threw up on the car floor.

Garth let out a slew of curse words.

"Dang, Naomi! This is a new truck!"

"You left my niece with gunmen!" she screamed, her

head still between her knees.

"I told you she'll be fine," he roared back.

Naomi wished she could believe him. But right now he sounded just as stupid as Charlie. Camille was not okay. And she wouldn't be until she was back home where she belonged.

If that ever happened.

Sobs choked her throat at the thought. He must have heard her, because she heard him sigh. "Look, I'm sorry. I know this is hard for you. It must have been hard to see Camille like that. But we'll get her. This time tomorrow, you'll be with your niece, I promise."

Naomi sat up slowly and looked over at him.

"You promise?"

He scowled at her. "Promise."

It was the first thing he had said since she arrived that she actually believed. At least that's what she told herself. After all, what other choice did she have?

Chapter Thirteen

Her head might have been aching but Naomi knew she wasn't at Latoya's place when they turned into the gated apartment complex on Stanmore Avenue, just a short distance from Victoria Square.

"Why have we stopped here?" Naomi asked as Garth pulled into a parking space and shut off the engine.

He got out of the SUV and opened her door before he answered.

"Because it's two in the morning and I am not about to go knock on Latoya's door at this time of the night," he said, as he offered his hand to help her out.

"So we're at....?"

"My place," Garth said. "You can stay here for the night and then I'll take you back up the hill in the morning."

Despite his outstretched hand, Naomi remained rooted in the vehicle. Going to Garth's place was not part of the plan. In fact, in the list of things that she should definitely never ever do ever again, being alone with Garth Duhaney was right up there at the top.

His hand dropped. "Or, if you feel like you can't control yourself, you can sleep in the car. This is a safe community. We have a twenty-four hour guard. You'll be fine."

He pulled the puke covered mat out the car and tossed it in a trash can nearby before he closed the door and walked away.

Naomi's mouth fell open. There was no way he would actually leave her there. Right?

She watched in disbelief as he turned the corner of the building and disappeared out of sight. Naomi unlocked her door and scrambled out of the car. She took off after him. She rounded the corner to find him leaning against the wall, laughing. She punched him hard in the chest.

"I can't believe you were going to leave me there."

He chuckled even as he rubbed his chest. "Hey, you're a grown woman, you make your own choices."

She followed him up to the second floor where he let her into his apartment. It was nice. New. Looked like he had kept all the furniture they staged it with.

"Look at you, all grown and responsible," she glanced back at him as he watched her appraise his place. "Rental?"

"Nope." Garth tossed his keys on the side table and locked the deadbolt on the door. "Owned outright. No mortgage."

Naomi raised an eyebrow at him. "How did you swing that?"

He smiled at her and winked. "You're not the only one who's changed, Nay."

She watched him with new eyes as he toed off his shoes and walked easily down the only hallway to a room she assumed to be his bedroom. A place she would be staying far away from.

To reinforce this thought in her mind, she headed in the opposite direction towards the kitchen.

"Make yourself at home," he called out from the bedroom. "There's drinks in the fridge. If you're lucky, you might find some leftovers from last night's dinner."

Naomi opened the fridge and peeked into a container. "Roasted chicken. Who cooked?"

She heard him laugh.   "Do you really want to

know?"

That answer was enough to give her a good idea. She closed the container and pushed it to the back of the fridge. She chose instead a bottle of iced tea. She had just finished pouring herself a glass when Garth returned to the room. The glass slipped from her fingers and landed noisily on the counter, but thankfully, only a few drops spilled onto the clean surface. Unfortunately, the damage of seeing a shirtless Garth as he walked towards her was a lot less harmless.

Naomi tried with every ounce of self-will she could muster to look away. But it was almost three a.m. and it looked like her will power had turned in for an early bedtime. She watched him watch her as he circled the counter. He sauntered directly into her space. Garth took the glass of iced tea from her and took a long sip. She knew he knew exactly what he was doing.

With her breath stuck in her throat, Naomi managed to look away long enough to retrieve the bottle of iced tea and return it to the refrigerator.

"Why are you doing this, Garth?" she asked, her back still to him as she took her time putting the tea back.

"Doing what?" he countered. She didn't miss the teasing tone in his voice. To him, it was all a game. Never mind the fact that her niece was probably lying in some stranger's bedroom right now. Naomi's commitment to her fiancé and the four years of celibacy she had struggled to make it through meant nothing to Garth who by all accounts had just had a woman in his apartment and likely in his bed less than twenty-four hours ago.

She walked around the kitchen island and away from Garth. "Never mind. Where is your spare room?"

"How do you know I have one?"

"Cause I know your mother," Naomi shot back, as she

headed towards the short hallway.

He chuckled. "First door on your right, across from the bathroom."

She headed straight for it. "Let me know when we are leaving."

Naomi closed the door firmly behind her, and leaned against it wearily.

"Thank you, God," she whispered towards the ceiling even as she realized that she hadn't prayed since she stepped off the plane. That would probably explain why her emotions had felt so chaotic all day. She thought it was Garth but maybe it was her. She had no idea what she was doing.

She slid down to the floor and closed her eyes. She knew she should pray something more substantial than the "Thank you, God" she had just offered up for being saved from Garth and herself, but she didn't know what. What would Jordan say? He would have the perfect eloquent words for a time like this. But Naomi couldn't think of what they would be. Furthermore she didn't want to think about what Jordan would say if he knew where she was right then.

"God, help me. I'm lost. I have no idea what I am doing and I feel like I have made a mess of things with finding Camille and everything else. Get me through this please. And please, please, please keep Camille safe."

Naomi had paused and tried to think of what else to say when a knock on the door startled her. She scrambled to her feet, but instead of opening the door, she just stood and stared at it, afraid of what waited for her on the other side.

The knock came again. "Naomi."

What would happen if she stayed here in this condo with Garth tonight? They had never slept in the same place together without sleeping together. And seeing him walk into that kitchen had flooded her with years of memories of just what that was like. It was amazing the things your memory held onto. And the things it chose to forget when it wanted to. Images, feelings, experiences you didn't even realize you still had with you until something triggered them to the surface. She could remember the feel of his skin. The rough spot on the right side of his lower ribcage where he had received a deep gash falling out of a mango tree. The tiny half-moon birthmark under his left collar bone where if she touched she could...

"Naomi, I know you're awake. Open the door."

Naomi chastised herself for her thoughts and yanked the door open. "What?"

"I thought you might want to sleep in something other than those," he nodded towards her black fitted pants even as he held out a pile of red jersey fabric.

Naomi let out the breath she held then lifted the item from his outstretched hand.

"Garth, I am not sleeping in one of your..."

She stopped short when the garment fell free and she realized what it was.

"It's not mine, as you can see," he said quietly.

Naomi turned over the familiar oversized shirt in her hands, speechless. She looked up at him then back at the red fabric.

"You kept this?" She stared at him. "Why?"

He shrugged. "Why wouldn't I?"

Naomi searched his eyes. She tried to understand the man who stood in front of her. But she had trouble putting all the pieces together. The Garth she remembered, the one who would rather have a drink than a serious conversation, the one who convinced her to defy her family but would never face them with her, the one who brought chaos with him when he showed up, was not the one who stared at her right now with melting, dark chocolate eyes. The Garth she knew would have never saved her t-shirt from four years ago. Truthfully, the Garth she knew would have left her in that apartment above the bar instead of coming back for her. But this guy was different.

"Thanks," she said, not quite sure how else to respond.

He nodded and stepped out of the doorway. "I'll see you in the morning."

She closed the door for a second time, and turned the lock after her. This time, it wasn't to keep Garth out, but more to keep herself in. Naomi started to realize, the person she trusted the least, was herself.

Chapter Fourteen

Naomi stared at Garth's ceiling for most of the early morning hours. She thought about everything, from her last moments with Camille, to the first time Nigel had brought her home. That had been the day after Camille's sixteen year old mother ducked out of the hospital without saying a word. No one had seen or heard from her since. How a mother could leave her child was incomprehensible to Naomi. But when the mother was a child, well, it made sense. She had watched her niece grow up, almost feeling like her mother as she babysat her, picked up after her when she got older, walked her to school and helped her with her homework. When Camille walked across the stage at her high school graduation, Naomi had cried as if Camille was her own child. And she had cried again when she packed her up and dropped her off at her dorm at Fordham. Now here she was, lying in bed, crying again for Camille, this time because she was throwing her life away.

How had she let this happen? Hadn't she done her best with Camille? Why would she think doing something this stupid was okay?

Maybe because of all the things she's seen you do.

Naomi turned to the side as if physically moving would evict the thought from her mind. The truth was, she hadn't always been a stellar example for Camille. Camille had seen what Naomi became when Garth had shown up in New York the first time. She had thrown her life away with little more than a second thought when Garth came looking for her. What kind of example had that been? And then, when Garth had shown up the second time, after her break-up with Jordan, Camille had been there too. Camille had witnessed Naomi's life circling the drain over a man. Latoya was right. She did have issues where men were concerned.

She twisted and turned under the light sheets and attempted to sleep, but was only able to achieve brief moments of semi-consciousness. When the first rays of dawn cracked the sky, she gave up trying and climbed out of bed.

Naomi's joints ached from exhaustion as she shuffled out of the bedroom to the kitchen. She pulled the fridge open again, and reached past the bottles of Heineken and Smirnoff for the iced tea. The cool sweet liquid felt welcomed down her throat. She leaned against the counter and pressed the chilled glass against her parched skin. Garth had air conditioning installed in the bedrooms. But out here in the main living space, she had to deal with the brutal summer heat.

"Couldn't sleep?"

She jumped a little and followed the sound of his distant voice to beyond the couch where the double glass doors in the living room opened up to a small terrace. One door slid open and he stepped back inside, still shirtless, holding an ice-filled glass of his own.

She shook her head. "Not really."

As he moved towards the kitchen, she saw the grogginess in his own half closed eyes. "Want to talk about it?"

With him? No.

"Would it kill you to have AC in the entire condo?" she asked before she finished the rest of her drink.

"It's only this bad, maybe one month out of the year." Garth shook an ice cube into his mouth as he leaned against the sink across from her. "You used to love the hot summers, Miss Savoy."

89

"That was before my body became Americanized." Naomi closed her eyes and pulled her hair off her neck with both hands.

She heard Garth shake the ice in his glass. "Then maybe you need to find a way to cool off."

Her eyes popped open. She sucked in a rapid breath as a cold, solid, block slipped inside the front of her jersey shirt, hitching in the front hook of her bra and sending trickles of icy water down her chest and stomach.

"Garth!"

She reached for her shirt to remove the ice cube but he clasped her wrists in his hands first. "Let it melt."

"It's cold!"

He pulled her closer to him. Suddenly, she was pressed against his hard chest. "That's the point."

She opened her mouth to protest, but her words got lost on his lips as his mouth crashed down on hers. His lips were still cool from the ice cube he had been sucking on. It had an interesting effect on her. She couldn't stop herself as she opened her mouth more to him. She deepened the kiss, allowed him to probe her mouth. Garth lifted her onto the counter. It was almost as if her mind blacked out to some dark place she had been before, but which she should have known better than to go back to. It was a place her body remembered well. Too well.

But Naomi had promised herself she would never go back there again. She would never go down this road again.

She had to stop.

But Garth touched her, in places that only he knew. It was almost as if for a moment she was paralyzed. Which seemed to work for Garth because he was all hands and action. It was like her twenty-first birthday all over again.

The day she let him take her away from New York back to this place. The day that changed her whole life.

This was way out of control. Correction. He was in control. And her body had switched to some kind of autopilot. Naomi couldn't seem to pull away from him. Couldn't stop him kissing her, couldn't stop him touching her and - Lord forgive her - couldn't stop a part of herself from wanting it.

But she had to stop. God help her, she had to stop.

"Here or back there?" He grunted the words against her neck.

"No," the word came out like a whimper, but it came out.

"Okay," His mouth returned to her skin. "We won't move..."

"No, stop," Naomi managed, a little louder than before. She pushed him back with her palms on his chest.

"Huh?" He was breathing hard, sweat glistened at his temples as he glared at her. "What are you talking about?"

"I can't," she shook her head and tried to move, but found herself trapped, with his solid frame between her legs and his palms on either side of her on the counter. "I can't do this, Garth."

"We're already doing it." His head dipped back to her neck. His hands gripped her arms. Hard. So hard it felt like his fingers were beginning to dig into her. Bolts of panic shot through her as she realized that she couldn't get away.

"Garth, stop. You're hurting me!" She struggled against him, but he ignored her and pressed in harder. His hands gripped tighter. When Naomi felt his teeth in her shoulder, she screamed.

"Stop!" she kicked hard, her toe landed somewhere soft.

He roared at the pain. His hand flashed out and knocked her hard on the side of her head. It hurt, but it loosened his grip on her enough for her to scuttle away. Naomi nearly fell backwards onto the floor as she pulled her legs up and backed off the counter onto the other side of the island. She figured this was safer than trying to go through him. She found she could breath easier when there was a heavy slab of marble between them.

She held the side of her aching head. "I can't believe you just hit me!"

"I can't believe you just kicked me."

Her eyes narrowed at him in disgust. "I don't know what I was thinking. We are so over."

He clenched and unclenched his jaw. "Didn't feel over a minute ago."

She picked up her shirt and pulled it over her head. "Maybe, but that will never happen again. Ever."

"Yeah, I've heard that before." Garth rubbed a hand over his face and turned his back to her for a moment. "Why won't you just admit it, Naomi?"

"Admit what?"

He turned around, his eyes seared into her. "That you still have feelings for me."

"Are you serious right now? You just hit me!"

"Look, I'm sorry. It was an accident...."

Naomi turned to walk away. "It's always an accident with you, Garth."

"Naomi, wait..." He grabbed her arm but she pulled away from his grasp.

"Don't touch me!"

They both stood in the middle of the living room

breathing hard. They stared at each other. It was then that Naomi understood clearly for the first time what she couldn't before. This was who Garth was. She always wandered back to him, hoping he would be different, hoping he had changed. But he never changed. Could never change. Not if he didn't want to.

He rubbed his hand over his face. "Come on, Nay. I know you feel it. Do you need me to say it first? Okay, I will. I still have feelings for you, Naomi. Me leaving New York was a mistake. We should still be together. We should have never…"

"No, Garth," Naomi cut in. "You're wrong. We were a mistake. Every time we are together, it hurts. It hurts me. How can that be right?"

"You're just trying to make excuses to be with that guy."

"That guy is my fiancé."

Garth snorted. "Well he must not be doing something right, because I have never seen you go from zero to sixty as fast as you did awhile ago."

"You have no idea what you're talk…"

Heavy knocking at the door interrupted Naomi. They both froze. They looked at each other then looked at the door. The knocking came again. It was barely six in the morning. Who would show up at Garth's door at this time?

Garth strode over to the door. "Who is it?"

Naomi drew a sharp intake of breath as Garth pulled a gun from the end table near the door and tucked it in the back of his waist.

"It's me," a rough male voice said from the other side. "Now quit playing and open this door."

Garth turned to Naomi, and jerked his head towards the bedroom. She slipped back into the guest room and pulled the door almost closed just as Garth opened the front door. She watched through the crack as a thick, dark skinned brother, shaved bald with an ugly scar along the side of his neck greeted Garth.

"Man, why you have me standing outside like a criminal," he asked so aggressively, Naomi wasn't sure he was joking. "What you doing in here?"

"It's six o'clock in the morning," Garth shot back. "What you think I'm doing?"

The man cracked a smiled and exposed platinum grilled teeth. "Knowing you? A lot of things."

Both men chuckled as they walked over to the living room out of Naomi's range of sight.

"So what you got for me?" Garth finally asked.

Naomi heard shuffling and assumed the man was opening the black duffel bag he had come in with.

"It's all here. Thirty-five Gs in twenties and..."

"Alright, alright," Garth cut him off. "I believe you."

They continued talking but Garth had lowered his voice. They were speaking so low Naomi had to strain to hear. She was able however to make out Garth's next question.

"You hear anything for me about the girl?"

"Listen, this one is rough," the guy said. "We didn't know she was a friend of yours, it's gonna be hard to..."

The AC in the bedroom kicked in and drowned out any chance of Naomi hearing what was said. She tried, but she couldn't make out the whispers. The next thing she knew, Garth's visitor walked towards the door. A few moments later, he left. As soon as he did, Naomi came back into the living room. She looked around but the duffel bag was gone. She had watched the man leave and knew he hadn't taken it with him. Garth hadn't had a chance to go back to his bedroom. It had to be in there somewhere. And for some reason, she was curious to see if in fact it was full of money as the overheard conversation had suggested.

"What was that about?" She asked suspiciously.

"Nothing," Garth answered from the kitchen where he washed his hands. "You want some breakfast? I got toast and eggs, but if you want more than that, we can stop on our way back to Latoya's."

Clearly their earlier conversation and encounter was briefly forgotten. That was okay with Naomi. She was more concerned about the real reason she had come to Trinidad in the first place - to find Camille.

"Did you find out anything more about Camille?"

Garth looked up at her curiously as he popped two slices of toast into the toaster. "You were eavesdropping."

"Of course."

He shook his head and chuckled as he took the butter from the fridge.

"They want to move her out today. We're gonna try and intercept them this morning." He pulled out a plate and a butter knife. "If we hit the house before they leave, we should be able to catch them. They're not expecting us."

"What time?"

"In about two hours."

Naomi headed back to the bedroom. "I'll go get ready."

"You're not going, Naomi."

She whirled around. "Excuse me?"

"I'm taking you back to Latoya's, then I'll go deal with this."

"You are not going to find my niece without me..."

"They already saw you last night," Garth said calmly as he pulled the slices from the toaster. "If they see you today, they'll know something's up. It could complicate things."

"Complicate things how?"

He buttered a slice and ate half with one bite. "It's just better for everyone. I can't look out for you and get your niece at the same time."

"I can look out for myself!"

"Like you did last night?" He asked, an eyebrow raised. He finished the rest of the toast then dropped the plate in the sink. "You're not going, Naomi. That's final."

"Garth, you can't just shut me out of this," she protested as he walked towards the bathroom. She followed him. "She is my niece."

"I'm not talking about this anymore."

She charged into the bathroom after him. "What if I refuse to get out? What are you gonna do, throw me out the car?"

He turned on the shower and removed his track pants. Naomi whirled around quickly and turned her back to him when she realized he was completely naked underneath.

"I think I can figure out a few ways to get you to do what I want," he said with amusement from behind her. "Now if you don't mind, I'm about to take a shower, unless you want to..."

Naomi darted out of the bathroom and pulled the door shut behind her before he could finish his sentence. She rubbed her hands over her face. So Camille was still alive, and Garth knew where she was. She knew what he said about her being a liability made sense, but she couldn't just sit back and wait for him to show up with Camille. She had to do something.

She walked back to the living room as she tried to think. Naomi glanced around. She remembered the missing duffel bag. She peered back down the hallway. The shower was still going. Hurriedly, she lifted up cushions, checked under the sofa and in the coat closet. Anywhere Garth could have hidden the bag. It was nowhere to be found in the living room or the small kitchen. The condo wasn't exactly huge, where could it be? She did another look around then caught sight of a door off to the right of the kitchen. A turn of the knob revealed a tiny laundry room, barely big enough to hold a washer and dryer stacked on top of each other. Naomi opened both and was rewarded when she found the black sack stuffed into the hollow of the dryer.

Her eyes widened when she opened it and found dozens of banded stacks of money. US dollars. She flipped through one stack of twenties and then another of fifties. She calculated in her head. There were at least twenty to thirty stacks in here. If each one held a thousand, there had to be at least...

"What do you think you're doing?"

Garth's hand clamped roughly around her arm. He yanked her up and out of the laundry room with one swift movement and slammed the door closed. After he shut the money inside, he turned his angry eyes on her.

"I invite you into my home and you disrespect me by searching through it?"

"What are you doing with all that money, Garth?" Naomi asked, as she ignored his anger. Garth was in to something. She knew it.

"What's in my house is none of your business."

"Are you running some kind of shady business?" she asked. "Getting kickbacks for looking the other way on some kind of police thing?"

"We're leaving," he said. Garth dragged her towards the guest room. "Get your stuff."

Naomi pulled out of his grasp and turned to look at him. "I can't believe I fell for it. I actually thought you had changed."

"It's you who changed, Naomi," Garth met her gaze. "You don't live here anymore. You forget what things are like here. You think everywhere is like New York and you see everything through the blinders of your American dream. Well, this isn't the US, sweetheart. And the only dreams that are worth anything here are the ones that you make happen for yourself."

Naomi shook her head. Her voice dripped with disappointment when she spoke. "What happened to you?"

"Life," he said dryly. "Now, unless you want to arrive at your cousin's wearing that scrap of a shirt, I suggest you get dressed."

Garth's eyes had grown dark. Naomi knew he wouldn't hesitate to throw her into his SUV with her dressed in nothing but the scrap of jersey material. She quickly pulled on her pants and grabbed her purse. Moments later, he ushered her out of the condo and down the stairs.

The drive back up to her cousin's place was quick and quiet. The early morning sun had crept in, and slowly warmed up the day, though the air remained frosty in the vehicle. When Garth finally pulled up to Latoya's gate, he disengaged the locks for her to get out, but she didn't move.

"Stop the foolishness, Naomi. The more time you waste here, the longer it takes me to get to your niece."

"It wouldn't take any time at all if you took me with you," Naomi folded her arms.

Instead of answering, Garth got out of his side then came around to the passenger side and opened her door.

"Last chance, Naomi."

"Garth, you can't expect me to just sit here and do nothing while you claim to be helping my niece..."

"Claim?" Garth's eyebrows shot up. "After all the hell I am going through for you, you don't even trust me?"

"There is thirty grand in US dollars in your condo that you won't explain," Naomi snapped. "Why should I trust you? I have a good mind to call the chief of police on your a-..."

Before Naomi could finish the thought, she felt herself yanked roughly out of the vehicle. She screamed as Garth flung her over his shoulder. She was really getting tired of him doing that.

"Put me down!" She tried to kick him, but he held her legs securely as he strode up the walkway and banged on the front door. She fought him in vain even as the door swung open.

"Where the hell have you been with my cousin!"

Naomi heard Latoya's voice but didn't see her until Garth deposited her on the floor inside the living room. She glared at him as she tried to right her clothes, which had become rumpled as he manhandled her.

"Ask her," Garth said in response to Latoya. "And make sure she tells you how she almost got herself killed last night."

Latoya turned angry eyes on Naomi. "Is that true? I told you going with him was a bad idea. And what happened to your clothes?"

Naomi pushed her hair out of her eyes. "What?"

"That's not the shirt you had on last night," Latoya's eyes widened. "Did you spend the night with him?"

Garth answered before she could. "What if she

did?"

"Naomi?"

All three of them turned towards the stairs, but Naomi was the only one who felt her heart stop beating. She had to be hallucinating. This could not be happening. There was no way...

Garth glared at the visitor on the stairs. "Who are you?"

"I'm Jordan. Naomi's fiancé." He stepped from the stairs onto the main level, his brows drawn tightly together as he took in the scene before him. Naomi felt herself shrink as his dark angry gaze settled on her before it shifted to Garth. "And who are you?"

"I'm Garth Duhaney." Garth smirked. "Naomi's husband."

Chapter Fifteen

"Ex-husband."

Naomi and Latoya said it at the same time but Jordan didn't even blink at them. He was too busy sizing up the man who stood in front of him. He determined quickly that he could take him if he had to. It just might end up happening after he put his fist through the man's face. He had seen him carry Naomi in through the door, seen the guilt hijack Naomi's eyes when she caught sight of him, noticed the marks on her neck that she probably hadn't given herself. Even if brother man hadn't announced it, he knew something had went on between the two of them.

But while he wanted to level Garth to the ground for the overly familiar way he looked at his fiancée, Jordan knew that Garth was not the problem. The secrets were. And there seemed to be more of them than he had earlier anticipated.

"You need to leave." He directed his statement to Garth in a much calmer tone than he thought possible for himself.

The man folded his arms across his chest and smirked at Jordan. "Or what?"

Jordan pushed up his sleeves as he walked across the room towards Garth. "There is no *or.*"

He watched Garth take him in. He evaluated his options then stepped back and moved towards the door.

"Whatever, I'm outta here anyway." He pulled open the front door, glanced back at Naomi and said, "I'll call you."

As soon as the door closed, Latoya headed towards the stairs. "I'll be upstairs if you need me. Try not to break anything."

Jordan waited until Latoya left the room before he looked at Naomi. The woman he had planned to spend the rest of his life with stood a few feet away from him. Her arms wrapped around her body as she shook. He had been so sure about her. So sure that they were meant to be together. But now he wasn't sure of anything at all. Each day seemed to prove that the woman he had proposed to, the one he thought he was in love with, didn't really exist at all.

"Start talking, Naomi."

He watched her run a hand through her wine tinted curls nervously. She was probably trying to pick through her lies, as she figured out which ones he knew and which ones she had managed to keep concealed.

"I came here because of Camille," she finally said. "She... when I told you I didn't know where she was...She's here. She came here with her boyfriend, Andre. She's swallowed pellets of cocaine to take back to New York. I just found out a couple days before and I came as soon as I could to see if I could find her..."

"Without saying a word to me."

Naomi looked away. "I didn't want to bother you with it... I just wanted to get her back and get back to New York as soon as possible."

"And what else didn't you want to *bother* me with Naomi?" he barked, as he stepped closer to her. "The fact that you have a brother who's in prison? The fact that Camille is your niece, not your sister? The fact that you were previously married?"

Naomi shrank back, tears filled her eyes. "I'm sorry. I should have told you but...."

"But you chose to lie to me instead," Jordan spat. "After everything we've been through, Naomi. After four years of being together, after the break-up, even through all the wedding plans, you looked at me and you lied to me. What else was a lie, Naomi?"

"Nothing else, that's everything," she cried, tears ran down her cheeks.

"Really?"

"Yes," Naomi nodded through her sobs "Yes."

"Did you sleep with him?"

She froze, her eyes widened as she stared at him.

He trembled as he watched her disintegrate into panic before his eyes. What would he do if she said yes? What would he do if he found out that the woman he loved with his body, heart and soul had given herself to another man in the last twenty-four hours? Could he live?

"Well, did you?"

Naomi sobbed again, quiet wailing sounds that ripped his heart to shreds. He couldn't take it. He didn't want to know. But he had to. He couldn't live past this moment without knowing the truth.

"Answer me!"

"No!" she screamed. "No! I didn't sleep with him. Okay? Is that what you want to hear? Yes, I spent the night at his place. Yes, he kissed me and touched me but I swear, that was it."

Jordan felt the moistness in his eyes as his heart shattered into a million pieces. Naomi had broken him. The woman he loved had bruised him beyond repair. Her words had given him no comfort, because in his heart he knew the truth.

"Maybe your body didn't get there," he said quietly. "But your mind already did. Were you ever really over him?"

"Yes," Naomi croaked through her sobs. "I was...I am...it was a mistake....just..."

She didn't finish. She didn't have to. Somehow, he understood the rest. He walked over and pulled her into his arms. She fell against his chest, her warm body fit into all the spaces that were just for her. She trembled against him. Jordan longed to hold her close, crush her in his arms, and keep her there forever. Instead, he kissed the top of her head gently as he drew in the scent of her then he pressed his lips to her ear.

"I don't think I know who you are..." Jordan's breath hitched in his throat. He could barely whisper the rest. "I can't...I can't marry you. This...us...it's over."

He heard her gasp, felt the air leave her body. Her hands tightened around him, but he pulled back and forced himself away even as he struggled to breathe. He couldn't stand the thought of being without her. But right now, Jordan couldn't be around her. It felt like she was sucking the life out of him. He eased her away and headed towards the door.

"Jordan!"

He opened the door and left.

Chapter Sixteen

"You have reached the voicemail of Garth Duhaney. Leave me a message and I'll..."

Naomi hit the end button before she heard the rest of the prompt then dropped the phone onto her lap.

"Still no answer?"

"No."

It had been four hours and seventeen unanswered calls to Garth since the man had walked out of Latoya's home. Everything that he said was going to go down with Camille should have happened two hours ago. She should have heard from him then, but there was nothing. By this time, her chest should have been tightening in panic but she was too numb to feel anything. When Jordan had whispered those final words in her ear, something inside her died.

I can't marry you.

Four years of togetherness, four years of promise, ended by those four words. He couldn't marry her. Wasn't that what she knew would have happened anyway? This was the inevitable end once everything came out. She should have been better prepared.

"...Naomi. Naomi!"

She barely registered Latoya until the woman yelled in her ear. She turned her head to look at her, and caught the look in her cousin's eyes. It was a mix of pity and concern.

"What do you want to do?"

Naomi turned her head towards the car window and

looked out at the people moving in and out of the airport doors. Checkered cabs taxied up to the doors to drop off more travellers even as others pushed luggage filled carts through the busy scene. Was her niece here? There was only one way to find out.

"Let's go find her."

They walked through the bustle, into the main doors towards the check in point. As they closed the distance, Naomi realized that getting past this level was going to be a challenge without tickets.

She had no choice. She stepped up to the counter.

The clerk smiled at her. "Welcome to Caribbean Airlines! Where will you be travelling today?"

"I have information on a possible drug smuggling operation happening today. I need to speak with someone."

The smile melted off the woman's face like a scoop of ice cream on hot concrete. Naomi saw her hand move under the counter. Moments later, two large men in uniform were standing behind her.

"Ma'am, can you come with us please?"

Sandwiched between the two men, Naomi made her way across the airport through a secured area, down several unmarked corridors past more uniformed individuals. The one who seemed to be in charge of all the talking flashed a key card over a security point. The previously red light on the door's magnetic port turned green. He pulled it open.

"If you would just..."

The sound of a single wail like a police siren echoed across the small airport. It interrupted his statement. There seemed to be a sudden flurry of movement. Naomi whirled around and looked for the source. She heard the screaming start the same time she saw him.

"Andre!"

There was no way he could have heard her as he sprinted across the airport customs area.

A dog and three uniformed officers chased after him. It didn't even seem like he heard the screams, which Naomi knew must have come from the woman face down on the floor while two officers held her firmly. Naomi felt the breath leave her body. It was her - it was Camille!

Her feet were already moving as she ran to where her niece writhed on the floor. She could hear her wails. Naomi felt her grief even as one of the officers placed a knee on Camille's back.

"Camille!"

She was halfway there when a hard force knocked her off her feet and landed her on the ground also. Before she knew what happened her own arms were being pinned painfully behind her.

"No, that's my niece! Please..."

"You know that woman?" the officer asked roughly. He didn't relax his grip on her in the slightest.

"Yes," Naomi sobbed. Tears choked back her explanation and blinded her as she tried to see where they took Camille.

"You're going to have to come with us then."

She was hauled to her feet and guided in the same direction as Camille and Andre, who was now in cuffs and being held by two large officers. She tried to see her niece's face, but she was ahead of her and practically being carried by the two officers.

"Camille! Camille!"

The woman didn't look back. Within seconds, they were in a secured hallway with several doors on each side. Naomi had a feeling they were going to separate them. She had to see her niece first. Had to make sure she was okay.

She yanked free of the officer and ran towards the younger woman. She barrelled into her frame.

"Camille, it's me. Look at me!"

The woman shrugged Naomi off and turned to look at her for the first time. She peppered Naomi with curses. "Get away from me! I don't know you. Don't try to bring me down with you."

Shock froze Naomi's features.

It wasn't her niece.

Before another thought could form, she was harshly yanked away from the woman and unceremoniously deposited in a small room with nothing but a metal table, a chair and a mirrored glass window. Despite the furnishings, she paced the floor of the small space. Where was Camille? Why was Andre here without her? Had he...?

No, she refused think about that.

But what if he had? What if her niece lay dead somewhere?

Her throat began to close up. She banged on the window.

"I need to talk to someone," she yelled. "Please! I know you can see me! I need to speak to someone now!"

Naomi banged on the glass some more. She even banged on the door. Nothing happened. No one came. She screamed and kicked over the chair. She shoved the table away and continued to bang. She had to find out what was going on. She wanted to talk to Andre. He knew what had happened to Camille and she needed to know. She also needed to put her hands around his neck and squeeze the life out of him for what he had done to her family.

She banged and screamed until her arms were sore. Then she slunk into a corner and closed her eyes, too tired to fight the tears that she had barely held at bay. They all poured out. She had failed. Really failed. And this time it hadn't just destroyed her own life, but Camille's as well.

She didn't know how long she lay sobbing in the corner. Ten minutes? Maybe twenty. It seemed like forever before the door finally opened. She heard footsteps cross the floor. The chair was picked up and righted in its place. Energy spent, Naomi didn't even look up. Unless they told her about Camille, she didn't care.

"Naomi. Get up."

Naomi didn't think anything else could have surprised her that day, but Jordan proved her wrong. She sat up slowly, blinked to clear the grit from her eyes and her mind. She wasn't sure if what she saw was real.

"Jordan? What are you doing here?"

"Camille is safe," he ignored her question. "She's been taken to a hospital and she's receiving care to deal with everything she's been through."

"But, how…I just saw them get Andre…she wasn't there."

Jordan leaned against the wall with his arms crossed. "Camille got sick after she took the first pellet, but Andre forced her to take more. She couldn't handle the full load so they used the other young woman you saw to carry the rest. Andre then sent Camille on a separate flight on her own while he went with this young woman. When I had Camille pulled off the flight, she told the authorities everything, ID'd Andre and the other smuggler and helped us take them all down."

Naomi leaned her head back against the wall and closed her eyes. So Camille was safe. Thank God. She sprung up as

Jordan's words registered.

"Wait, you had Camille pulled off the flight? Not Garth?"

Jordan's eyes met hers for the first time since he had entered the room. They were dark and cold.

"Your friend, Garth, paid the customs officer to look the other way when Camille went through so that even though she looked sick as a dog, they let her on the flight," he frowned.

"But he told me he was going to help her. Get her to safety."

"And maybe he would have, after she arrived in New York, passed out the pellets, and he got his cut from making it happen."

Naomi felt her stomach drop.

"He was in on it?" she whispered.

"Probably not at first," Jordan ground out. "But somewhere along the way..."

Naomi closed her eyes and sobbed again. Sobbed for how wrong she had been for trusting Garth. How wrong she had been for not trusting Jordan, but how God had taken care of her niece anyway. Jordan remained quiet from his vantage point near the door. He didn't leave, but he didn't come any closer either.

"There are a couple of men here who will take you to the hospital to see her," Jordan said. "After that, I've made arrangements for both of you to travel back tomorrow morning. I think your mother would prefer to have you all home sooner rather than later."

Naomi sniffled and nodded. When he opened the door to leave, she had the frightening feeling that it would be the last time she saw him. She couldn't let him leave like this.

Not after everything he had done for Camille. For her.

She opened her mouth. "Jordan, thank you."

But by the time she got the words out, he was gone.

Chapter Seventeen

Camille's hospital room was in the west wing of the Community Hospital of Seventh-day Adventists in Port of Spain. Jordan must have pulled some more strings because she was in a spacious private room with its own balcony and a nice view of the hills through the window. At this end of the floor, it was quiet. In fact, the only sound Naomi heard as she sat at Camille's bedside was the whirring of the fan overhead.

She stroked her niece's hand as she took in the full view. She looked a little better than she had the last time she saw her, crumpled on the floor in the apartment above the bar. Still, the IV in her arm told Naomi that Camille wasn't completely recovered. Yet, the look in her eyes was hopeful.

"You must be spitting mad at me right now," Camille said, her voice quiet but laced with guilt.

Naomi sighed. "I am. But I'm more glad that you're here. Alive. Safe. When I saw you in that room passed out..."

Naomi couldn't finish, but the pressure of Camille's hand as she squeezed Naomi's told her that her niece understood the rest.

"I've been so stupid," Camille said with a groan. She covered her face with her free hand. "I can't believe I let Andre talk me into coming here with him."

"I don't understand," Naomi shook her head as she stared at Camille. "You are so smart, so independent, so no-nonsense. How could you let Andre talk you into this?"

Camille shrugged and looked away. But Naomi didn't

112

miss the tears that welled up in her Camille's eyes.

"I loved him," she sniffled. "And he said he loved me. I thought he loved me. Until I got here and he told me what he wanted me to do."

"Why didn't you just take off?" Naomi asked.

Camille choked back a sob. "I couldn't! Where would I go? I don't know anyone here. And when a guy dressed in a policeman's uniform came to the house to see Andre that first day, I knew, even if I did run, that I couldn't even trust the police. Besides, Andre had my passport. I was trapped."

"Mercy." Naomi pressed her niece's hand to her cheek as she thought of everything that could have happened to Camille.

"Naomi, I was so scared," Camille said. "I thought I was going to die. When you showed up, I was so relieved. But then they caught you and I wasn't sure whether you were dead or alive. And when I couldn't swallow all the pellets, Andre started to get mad. He..."

She stopped then as sobs robbed her voice and tears ran in rivulets down her face.

Naomi looked out the huge window. "He hit you, didn't he?"

She saw her niece nod out of the corner of her eye. "How did you know?"

Naomi sighed and turned her eyes on her niece. "Because we are more alike than we both realized."

"I couldn't believe he would do that to me," Camille tried to wipe away the tears. "How could he do that to me when he said he loved me?"

"Because he didn't love you, sweetheart," Naomi stroked her niece's hand. "Love wouldn't hurt you like that. Love wouldn't ask you to put yourself in danger like that."

She sighed. "Love would respect you and your choices instead of seeking after just what it wanted."

"When I saw Garth, I thought for a minute that he would help me," Camille said. "But he didn't. He told me I would be okay, but then he left me to get on the plane, knowing what was going on. If it wasn't for Jordan..."

"Yeah. I heard what he did for you."

Camille squeezed Naomi's hand, urging her to meet her eyes.

"He saved me."

Naomi couldn't stop the tears that rolled down her cheeks.

"I am so glad you brought him here. He's a good man."

Naomi nodded, not having the will to correct her niece. "The best kind."

Later when Camille had drifted off to sleep, Naomi slipped out of the chair by the bedside and slid the glass doors to the balcony open. Outside, the early morning summer sunshine blazed down on the balcony. Its heat only slightly abated by the cool Caribbean breezes that floated by. Naomi took in a deep breath. She wished that the fresh air would be enough to blow away all the confusion in her life. All the mistakes she had made and continued to make. More than anything else, she just wanted a fresh start.

She heard the sliding doors open but didn't turn around. She already knew who it was. His fresh scent of sandalwood and detergent was unmistakable.

"I didn't think I'd see you again."

Jordan leaned against the railing a few feet away from her. "I just came by to drop off the tickets for you and Camille. My flight leaves in a couple hours."

Naomi nodded but didn't look at him. Couldn't bear to

114

see the disappointment and hurt that probably lived on his face. She was just content to feel him near her, if only for a moment.

"How did you find out?" she finally asked.

"Natasha," Jordan answered. "Don't be mad at her. She was worried about you."

"I'm not," Naomi said. "She told me she wouldn't lie for me. Considering the circumstances, I'm glad she didn't."

"How could you lie, Naomi?" Jordan willed her to look at him. "How could you lie to me?"

The look he pierced her with broke her heart all over again.

"I didn't plan to," She looked away. "It's just that...I never thought we would get here, to the point where you would want to marry me. And then when it happened, it was almost like it was too late."

She pushed away from the railing and paced the small space. "I knew that if you knew, if everything about me was right there, you could never love me..."

"That's not true."

"Really?" Naomi whirled around to face him, "If the day you met me - that evening at the barbecue - if you had known that I was an alcoholic, divorcee with a brother in jail, would you still have asked me out? Would you?"

She saw his jaw tense. "I don't know."

"Well, I do." Naomi said. "You wouldn't have. You would have rightly branded me a train-wreck and ran the other way."

"So your plan was to deceive me?"

"No, my plan was to enjoy the night I had talking to the most handsome, intelligent and interesting man I had ever met, knowing that that was all it would be - one night. Because sooner or later, Charlie would let it slip or you would run into someone who knew, and then you would know."

Jordan stepped closer. "Know what?"

"Know that I'm a mess," Naomi said. "That a woman like me doesn't belong in your world."

"But don't you see, Naomi? You never gave me the chance to know that woman. Maybe I could have loved her. Maybe not." He threw his hands up. "I don't know. All I know is that the woman I thought I was in love with, she doesn't exist. And you?"

He waved his hand towards her and shook his head. "I don't even know who you are."

His words cut through her, but the look in his eyes hurt even more. It was as if he encountered a stranger - and not a welcomed one. That connection that had flown so easily between them had been severed. They were no more than two people who stood on a hospital balcony and stared at each other.

Jordan shook his head. "I need to go."

She wanted to stop him. Wanted to tell him that he was wrong. He did know her. The real her. The one deep inside. But how could she tell him that when she had spent four years keeping secrets from him? And how could it ever be different when the truth - the whole, unfiltered truth was too much for even her to speak? And so she watched him walk away. Watched his toned form disappear through the hospital doors, taking with it a piece of her heart.

Chapter Eighteen

Naomi cracked open the seal on the colorful clothbound notebook once the plane had leveled after take-off. She glanced over at Camille who was already asleep in the seat beside her. Her lashes rested softly on her smooth caramel colored cheeks. She was looking better each day. Except for the band aid on her arm where the IV had been, you couldn't tell that anything had been wrong at all. But so much had been wrong. With Camille. With her. With all of them. There were so many wounds that still needed healing. That's what the journals were for. But she had drifted away from them for a while. Maybe it was time she started back.

She wrote the month and year on the inside cover then turned to the first page. This one was different. It had a Bible text at the top of each page. Trust Latoya to get her something like this. The one at the top of the first page was 2 Corinthians 5:17.

Therefore, if anyone is *in Christ,* he is *a new creation; old things have passed away; behold, all things have become new.*

Naomi sighed. She didn't feel new right now. In fact, all the feelings that flooded through her felt like the same ones she had dealt with before. She uncapped her pen and began.

He left me. The only man that ever allowed me to be me and not feel bad about it. The man that taught me what real love looks like - he's gone. And I ran him away.

She continued writing. Naomi poured out the words in a way she never would have even to Natasha. The truth was she didn't know how to be this honest with anyone. She had spent so much time reserving pieces of herself from the people around her that she didn't know how to show it all.

She couldn't be sure that if she showed it all people would stick around. If they knew the dark parts, the messy parts, would they still love her? She didn't think so. There was only so much people could take. But on these empty pages, there was no judgment. Her words were just words. And on these pages she could release them into freedom.

Her fingers flew over the pages until her hand ached and she was too tired to write anymore. Naomi laid her head back and joined Camille in a shallow, unsettled sleep.

She didn't open her eyes again until the wheels touched the tarmac in New York. The landing jolted her awake. She sat up suddenly, looked around and found Camille watching her, a slight smile on her lips.

"Dreaming about Jordan?"

Naomi shifted in her seat and blinked rapidly. "Why?"

Camille grinned. "Cause you said his name a couple times...and not in an unhappy way."

Naomi felt her cheeks heat up in embarrassment. Okay so maybe he had made an appearance.

"Looks like we're here," Naomi ignored her niece's smirk as she glanced out the window.

"Yeah." Camille's smile waned. "Home sweet home."

"Don't sound so excited," Naomi said dryly.

"No, I am glad to be back," Camille said. "It's just...well...mom is gonna kill me."

Naomi shrugged. "After everything that happened, you should be glad that an earful from mom is all you have to deal with."

"You're right," Camille said. "Things could have been so much worse. Everything was so out of hand..."

"Yes, it was," Naomi said. "And I don't want that to

happen again, which is why some things are gonna change."

Camille looked hesitant. "What kind of things?"

"Well for one, I want you to start seeing someone," Naomi said. "You've been through a lot in your life with your dad being in prison and your birth mom taking off on you. I took it for granted that you were okay, but I think it would be good if you could talk to someone to help you work through it."

"You mean like a shrink?" Camille asked skeptically. "Black people don't do that."

Naomi rolled her eyes. "Well, you can be the first."

Camille let out a sigh. "Okay. What else?"

"I want you to come live with me."

"As in move off campus?" Camille screeched.

"Yes," Naomi confirmed. "I feel like I never see you anymore but if you are living with me at least we will get to spend more time together."

"You mean you will get to keep an eye on me," Camille said dryly.

"That too," Naomi said. "When you get tired of my mug you can go stay with mom in Jersey. But for now, my place will be your place."

"And how does your husband-to-be feel about all this? I am sure he can't be thrilled to have his sister-in-law up in his newlywed bliss."

Naomi stood up and reached for her luggage in the overhead compartment. "Jordan and I aren't getting married anymore so you don't have to worry about that."

Camille's mouth hit the floor.

"And by the way, he knows everything."

"Nigel and prison and Garth, everything?" Camille squeaked.

Naomi sighed and pulled down Camille's luggage. "Everything."

"Wow." Camille stood slowly and reached for her luggage. "Nay, I'm so sorry. If I hadn't done this..."

"It's not your fault," Naomi followed the other passengers towards the exit. "Believe me. It would have ended this way eventually. But on the bright side, I'll have a lot more time to spend with you now..."

"You mean to scrutinize my life now," Camille grumbled.

Naomi threw a smile behind her. "Exactly."

They followed the passengers out the plane and down the concourse towards the arrival gate. But as soon as they stepped into the arrivals area, Camille grabbed Naomi's arm.

"I'm really sorry about you and Jordan, Nay," Sincerity brimmed in Camille's eyes. "I know you really loved him."

Naomi blinked back the tears that threatened. She wouldn't cry in front of Camille. Partially because she didn't want the young woman feeling guilty but also because she wasn't sure that if she started that she could ever stop.

"It's okay." Naomi shrugged. "It will work out. It always does."

They wheeled their luggage through the airport crowds. If she had been travelling with Jordan, it would have been easy for Naomi to get through customs quickly as he had so many friends at the airport. Thinking back, Jordan should have been the first person she called when Camille took off. Indeed, hindsight was 20-20.

They were almost at the taxi stand when an image on the TV screens throughout the airport caught her eye. She stopped so suddenly that Camille slammed right into her with her suitcase. But Naomi was so glued to the television, she barely noticed. The sound was muted, but the images on the screen were easy enough to read.

"Is that Garth?" Camille asked as they stared up at the footage of a man being hauled away in handcuffs by the police. The caption read "Police officer in Port of Spain, Trinidad, taken in on corruption charges related to drug trafficking."

"Yeah, that's him." Naomi said quietly. She felt Camille shudder next to her.

"I hope they lock him up and throw away the key," she said with disgust. "I never want to see him again."

Naomi took one last look at the screen. She put an arm around Camille and turned her towards the exit.

"You and me both, kiddo."

And for the first time in years, she knew she meant it.

Chapter Nineteen

The sun was warm out on the front steps of Street Life, but Naomi was in a sweater. She felt chilly, exposed, as she sat out there all alone. But she couldn't bear to be inside either.

On the outside, everything seemed back to normal. The magazine ran like a well oiled machine, almost as if nothing had happened. When Naomi took the stairs down fifteen minutes earlier, Natasha was stomping around, giving everyone hell and making sure the next issue was a best selling one.

Naomi received a text message from her mother that confirmed Camille had shown up for her counseling session earlier that morning. Both, her mother and Camille would be going to see Nigel later that afternoon. They had a lot to talk about. Nigel especially had a lot to say to Camille about how he ended up where he was. It was time they stopped sheltering her so much.

She had heard from Latoya that Andre had been locked up in Trinidad for drug trafficking and the drugs they had taken out of Camille had been turned over to the police. Either way, he would not be back in New York for a long time, if ever.

Everything was right. Except for things with Jordan.

Jordan.

He was the reason she sat on the front steps of her building instead of being productive. He was the reason she couldn't focus. Couldn't think. Couldn't eat. Couldn't sleep.

She stretched her legs out in front of her and pulled the

cardigan tighter. New York in the summer. It was beautiful in its own way. Kids played on the sidewalk, cyclists shared space with motorists and pedestrians, AC units and car radios hummed. Everything seemed so alive.

Last year, she and Jordan had snuck away on a lot of these summer evenings. Once, they had taken the aerial tram to Roosevelt Island where they visited Four Freedoms Park and played hide and seek around the ruins of the Smallpox Hospital at the Southern end of Southpoint Park. Another time they used some free passes to spend a long lunch at the Bronx Zoo and saw the gorillas and polar bears. Naomi smiled as she thought about how much she would look forward to their spontaneous adventures. She would often have nothing more than an hour's notice for something as random as a ride on the Staten Island Ferry or as simple as a snow cone on the front steps. No matter what it was, she was happy because she was with him.

"Playing hooky?"

Naomi looked up. Amanda stood in front of her. Lost so deep in her thoughts, she hadn't noticed the woman walk up.

"Well, I am the boss, so technically, I can do what I want."

Amanda sat down beside her. "How's Camille?"

"Humble," Naomi said. "I think being held at gunpoint and having to get pellets removed from her stomach managed to smack the reality into her."

Naomi had confided to Amanda about what happened with Camille not long after she had apologized profusely to the woman for the cancelled wedding arrangements.

Amanda nodded. "Your mother must have freaked."

"She did," Naomi said. "She laid into Camille as soon as she stepped into the house. But when she finished, she cried and hugged her. What happened really scared Camille but I think she's going to be alright."

"And you?" Amanda squinted at her friend. "How are you doing?"

Naomi stared out ahead of her. Three little girls played jump rope across the street.

"Ask me again next week."

Amanda nodded. "If it helps, Jordan looks just as bad as you do. Maybe worse."

It didn't help. Naomi never wanted Jordan to get hurt. She could still see the look in his eyes from that day on the hospital balcony. It haunted her in ways she could never forget.

"I'm surprised you're even here talking to me," Naomi said. "I can't imagine how much embarrassment and expense this whole shenanigan cost your family."

Amanda shrugged. "It's just money. That comes and goes. We told everyone that there was a family emergency so the embarrassment was minimal. The parents still don't know exactly what happened though. I think Jordan and I have agreed to keep it that way."

Naomi turned to look at Amanda for the first time. "I'm really sorry. About everything. I'm sorry I hurt your brother, lied to you, and put your family through all of this. I just..."

"How could you have lied like that, Naomi?" The edge in Amanda's voice made Naomi look up at her. It was the first time since everything had happened, that she saw the full breadth of Amanda's feelings. "I know everyone has secrets, but Jordan was always so honest with you. How could you say you love him and keep all that from him?"

Naomi looked away as her eyes filled up.

"You know I never really thought me and Jordan could

last," Naomi said with a sigh. "I thought we would go out a few times and then we'd see how different we were and he'd lose interest. I never thought I would fall in love with him, and I definitely never thought he would fall in love with me. And when it happened, I wanted to tell him. I really did. But it was so… hard."

Naomi stood up and paced. "But I guess he already knew. All this time he knew about Nigel and he never said anything…"

"He was waiting for you to tell him."

"Maybe he was testing me," Naomi wondered out loud. "Guess I failed."

"He bought a house. He bought a ring. He was going to marry you," Amanda said. "In spite of what he knew, what you didn't tell him, he was still going to marry you. Does that sound like a test to you?"

Naomi stopped pacing.

"No," she finally admitted. "Not at all."

She sank back down onto the step. "I guess it doesn't matter anyway. All that is in the past. Jordan and I are in the past. And to be honest, I am kind of relieved. It was hard living up to the image he had of me."

"That's a load of crap and you know it," Amanda said. "You are not relieved. You miss him like hell."

Naomi sighed. Amanda was right.

"This whole thing is really hard for me," Amanda frowned. "He's my brother and you're my friend. You were a bridesmaid in my wedding. I love you like family. But he is family. And if it comes down to it, I choose him."

"I know." Naomi's eyes fell to the concrete. Amanda touched her arm. She looked up.

"But I honestly hope it doesn't come to it," Amanda

said softly. "This whole thing is a mess but at least it helped you both take each other off the pedestals you had each other on. You both needed to learn to love each other while acknowledging all the flaws between the both of you. So the person you fell in love with turned out to be less than perfect. That's life. It doesn't change how much you love them."

"It doesn't matter anyway," Naomi propped her chin on her folded arms. "I'm sure he's moved on."

"Stop fishing and just ask," Amanda rolled her eyes. "No, he's not seeing anyone. Especially not your skanky friend, Charlie, though she's been coming around and dropping bait."

Naomi shook her head. So what Natasha had told her about Charlie making a play for Jordan was true. No wonder she had barely laid eyes on her friend in the month since the wedding had been called off.

"You know she thinks that if I hadn't shown up at that barbecue four years ago, she and Jordan would have ended up together," Naomi said dryly.

"Are you serious?" Amanda said wide-eyed. "You let her say that to your face and still be walking upright?"

"She said it to Jordan. He told me, then asked me why we were still friends," Naomi recalled the conversation they'd had when she told him who her bridesmaids were going to be.

"Well, let me put all of that nonsense to bed for you," Amanda said. "My brother was taken with you long before the invitations for that barbeque ever went out."

Naomi turned to look at Amanda in surprise.

"Remember that Thirty under Thirty gala where you gave the speech about how the award helped you build all this?" Amanda motioned to the building behind them.

"Yeah," Naomi said.

"Remember that floor-length orange dress with the very low back?" Amanda asked. "My brother spotted you the minute you walked through the door. He couldn't take his eyes off you all night."

Naomi's eyes widened. "I didn't even know he was there! Why didn't he speak to me that night?"

"You know why."

Naomi thought about it a moment then smiled. She did know why. Because that was Jordan. He never got into anything major without doing his research and having a plan first.

"So he thought I was something major," Naomi smiled.

"Girl, you would not believe how he twisted my arm to get you invited to that barbecue," Amanda said with a laugh. "I don't know what he would have done if you had decided not to show."

So Jordan had been serious from the start. Even when they had dated only occasionally, he had already known how he felt about her. Naomi sighed and put her face in her hands.

"It's too late," Naomi groaned from behind her hands. "He said he doesn't even know me. And he's right."

Amanda squeezed Naomi's arm again. "Then maybe it's time you introduced yourself."

Chapter Twenty

The air was warm and filled with the scent of sweet alyssums as Naomi stepped through the heavy metal door. The sound of the city was nothing but a distant hum as she walked the stone pathway across the rooftop garden. The skinny needled blue star junipers that looked like chia pets the last time she was here now resembled beautiful blue-green oversized hedgehogs as they lined the path that led deeper into the garden. They were not the only things that had grown. Everything was coming in fuller than before, with a carefully tamed wildness that accompanied a mature garden.

Naomi found Ilana near the pergola pruning away the Japanese wisteria, the vines of which had spread in a network across the top and sides of the pergola, adding a beautiful covering of violet flowers to the covered sitting area. The beauty did not deceive Naomi however. She had been here long enough to know that if left untamed, the wisteria would take over the entire garden, which explained why Ilana was always so fastidious about keeping it in check.

"Still fighting your battle with the wisteria I see," Naomi drew closer.

"It is a continuous struggle," Ilana clipped away with her shears. "Sometimes I win, sometimes she does."

Naomi leaned against the side of the pergola. "Well, it looks like you have her in line today."

Ilana sighed and put down her shears. "I can only hope."

Then she turned to Naomi and smiled. "It's been a long time, my dear."

She opened her arms and Naomi fell into them. Ilana was small, her head barely reached Naomi's chin. But when she hugged her, Naomi felt all the warmth in the world. She squeezed back the tears that sprang to her eyes.

"Too long," Naomi whispered. "I am sorry I didn't return your calls."

Ilana let her go and shrugged. "It is what it is. You did not like what I had to say. I understand."

Naomi let out her sigh. "But you were right, Ilana. I wasn't ready. I'm still not."

Instead of answering, Ilana tucked her hand in Naomi's and led her to the wrought iron table and benches under the pergola. There was already a tray with tea and snacks set out. And when she touched the teapot to pour for each of them, it was still warm.

"I am glad you decided to come today," Ilana said as she tipped honey into her teacup and stirred. "When Rhea told me that you called and made an appointment, I thanked God for answered prayers."

Naomi stopped stirring her own tea and stared. "You were praying for me?"

"I pray for all my children, my dear," Ilana said. "Especially the ones I know are still hurting."

Naomi's eyes fell to her lap. "He called off the wedding, Ilana."

The woman took a sip from her tea. "What happened?"

"Garth."

"Ahhh," Ilana said as she put her teacup on the table. When she looked up at her, Naomi could see the sadness in the woman's eyes. Her sadness. The sadness they both carried for everything that the past held. "So, he found out."

"Yes." Naomi told the whole story from the first

suspicion that Camille was missing, to the drama in Trinidad, to sending back the wedding ring, which she had done the week after she came back to New York. As she told that part she couldn't help but look down at her left ring finger. It still felt light from the absence of the proof of Jordan's love.

Naomi shook her head. "You were right. I wasn't ready to get married. Not with everything in my past. Maybe I'll never be ready."

"So you have given up then?"

"No...yes..." Naomi pressed her fingers to her eyes. She didn't want to cry. Not anymore. She had cried a million tears already. But it seemed like she wasn't done yet. "I don't know if it's worth trying anymore."

She dropped her hands. "How could I let Garth do this to me? Again? After everything, how could I let him...what is wrong with me?"

She couldn't stop the tears now, or the sobs that choked her throat as she sat in the middle of Ilana's beautiful rooftop garden and faced the ugliness of her life.

She felt the air shift next to her. Arms encircled her as Ilana slipped onto the bench and pulled her into another embrace. Naomi willingly leaned against her shoulder. She bawled like it was the first time her life had fallen apart instead of the fifth or sixth. It seemed no matter what she did, she always ended up back here at rock bottom.

Ilana stroked her hair and rocked her gently in her arms. She hummed something that Naomi didn't recognize. Whatever it was, it calmed her. Her sobs subsided.

"You know when my Nathan was alive this whole garden used to be covered," Ilana said. "It was one big pergola covered in lattice. Of course, there were parts you could open and he did open them during the summer and spring. But he liked having the option to close it. Said it kept the birds from eating his flowers."

Naomi sat up from Ilana's arms and looked around at the large open space, unable to imagine it completely covered over the way Ilana described. "What happened to it?"

"After Nathan died, I took it all down," Ilana said.

Naomi looked over at the woman in surprise.

"I know," Ilana said with a wave of her hand. "I loved that man, rest his soul, but I hated the garden feeling like a prison, so I had it all ripped down, and left just this little part covered."

"Anyway, before it all came down, we used to have lots of birds come by. They would fly around over the top of the garden and come inside when the openings were left down all through the spring and summer, then they took off late fall and winter. Well, most of them anyway,"

Ilana sat forward. "You see those two over there?"

Naomi squinted in the direction where Ilana pointed and saw moving bursts of bright color. "Those yellow ones?"

"Those are my goldfinches," Ilana said proudly. "I'm not completely sure, because I don't know that much about birds, but I am sure they've been in this garden for years."

Naomi raised an eyebrow. "Years?"

Ilana nodded. "I am almost certain. You see, before the lattice came down we would have lots of birds fly through here and get trapped. Maybe Nathan would close the openings too early one day, or they would just hang around but not be able to find their way out when they tried to leave. We always had at least three or four stuck in here. When we had the lattice removed, I was sure they would fly away. But those two never did. We have had whole flocks of finches come through for a season then move on. It's what finches do. But those two never left. Never flew beyond the height of the pergola, never strayed beyond the bounds of the walls." Ilana tilted her head to the side thoughtfully. "The barriers are gone, but it's as if they are still there for them."

When she didn't say anything more, Naomi turned towards Ilana and found that the older Messianic Jewish woman watched her.

"I think, my dear, that you are like my little goldfinches." She touched Naomi's arm gently. "You are free, but you act as if you are not. The pergola of hurt that Garth put on you is gone. He is gone. But you have built up walls and ceilings of shame for yourself. You live in your shame, my dear, and it has imprisoned you."

Naomi closed her eyes as the cold reality of the truth washed over her. Was that what she was doing?

"I want to hate him, Ilana," Naomi whispered. "And a part of me does. But a part of me remembers who he was, the good and the bad. And I guess... I think...maybe, it was me. Maybe if I was different..."

She felt Ilana touch her chin. Naomi opened her eyes to meet her gaze. "You think if you were different that what? That Garth would not have hurt you the way he did? That he would be a different person?"

Ilana grabbed her hands tightly. "This is not your fault, Naomi. Who he is, that is not your fault, nor is it in your power to fix. You don't need to feel ashamed because of what he did to you."

"I should never have called him." Naomi shook her head. "I should never have let him back into my life, let him touch me. Why did I let him touch me, Ilana? Why did my body still..."

"Because you are human," Ilana said. "Because you once

knew this man intimately and your body remembers that. But your mind is a different place. And your mind chooses what you do. Yes, it was a bad decision to put yourself in a position to be alone with him like that again. But forgive yourself and let it go. God has already forgiven you, my dear."

Naomi shook her head, as the lump crawled back up her throat. "I know. I just don't feel it...I feel so...." she sighed as the word came back again. "I feel so ashamed."

Ilana turned her face to look at her again. "You have to let it go, my dear. Romans 8 tells us clearly there is therefore now no condemnation to them who are in Christ Jesus, who walk not after the flesh but after the Spirit. You have surrendered to Him so do not be led around by your flesh, by your feelings. You have to depend on the Spirit to guide you. And you have to believe that you have been made whole despite how you may feel. Feelings are a trick of the enemy. But God's word is true. And His word says that if any man is in Christ, he is a new creation. You are that new creation. You just have to believe it."

That had always been the hard part for her. Believing it. Believing that Christ had truly forgiven her for what she had done. Believing that she had no reason to be ashamed in Him. Believing that she was valuable in spite of everything in her past.

"I want to believe," Naomi whispered.

Ilana pulled her closer and Naomi laid her head on the woman's chest.

"Dear God, I present to you your child, Naomi," Ilana prayed. "Your precious jewel. One for whom You died. Help her to know how much You love her. Help her to accept fully the new life she has in You. And help her to let go of her shame. Heal her in her broken places, and make her whole. I give her into Your hands, amen."

Naomi didn't feel immediately different. There was no rushing wind that blew all her doubts away. But something did change. Somewhere in the depth of her heart, she decided to believe. Despite her feelings, despite what the past told her. She had been saved. She was forgiven. That would never change and she was never going back. And as she talked some more with Ilana, the weight that she had been carrying around for weeks seemed to slowly ease away.

"I can't believe it's been six months since the last time we talked like this," Naomi shook her head as they walked together through the garden. "I was so mad when you weren't happy about my engagement to Jordan."

"It was never about you and Jordan, my dear," Ilana said "I believe he is a good man. But secrets tear people apart. And you were not ready to share yours."

"Looks like they ended up coming out anyway."

Ilana looked across at her. "Did they?"

Naomi frowned.

"There is a story only you can tell, Naomi." Ilana said. "You have to be willing to tell that story."

Cold washed over Naomi as she thought about Ilana's words and then about her conversation with Amanda. Jordan thought he knew her. But even with what he had recently learned, Naomi realized he still didn't really know her. He knew facts about her - she had finally given him that much - but she still hadn't let him know her completely.

Ilana rubbed Naomi's arm where small goose bumps arose. "It is okay to be afraid. But perfect love casts out all fear. If his love for you is true, then it will not change with the truth."

Naomi knew that. She knew the kind of man Jordan was. He would never blame her for anything she told him. The problem wasn't with him - it was with her. How could she relive a truth to someone else that she was too afraid to face herself?

Chapter Twenty-One

Naomi hated basements.

She wasn't sure if it was the claustrophobic feel of a room with lower ceilings and no windows, or the fact that they reminded her of the cellar under their house in Trinidad where her brother had threatened to lock her when they were little. Whatever it was, she avoided basements as much as possible. Even when she sold her house and had to store her furniture in the basement of the Street Life building, she had stood at the top of the stairs and supervised the process from there rather than come down into the basement itself.

But here she was nonetheless, back in that same basement. And this time, she would have to go a little further than the top of the stairs.

She hit the switch and fluorescent lighting illuminated the large unfinished space. To the right were old media materials, boxes of archived issues of the magazine, and clunky promotional materials from trade shows and events. To the left were couches, lamps, a couple end tables and boxes upon boxes of Naomi's life. These should have been moved to the house that Jordan had closed on three months earlier. But it seemed like they would have to stay put for the foreseeable future. She headed left stepping over a hassock and a crate marked fragile before she found what to she was looking for.

It was still there.

A layer of dust covered the polished wooden surface and the combination lock that secured the contents inside. It hadn't been opened in a long time. Even before it had come to rest in the Street Life   basement. But now it had to be.

Even as she stood in front of the box, knowing what she needed to do, Naomi couldn't make herself move. She couldn't even make herself reach for the box. Just the thought of letting everything out...

Her head felt light. She sank down onto the crate marked fragile, forgetting about its contents. She sat there, made herself breathe normally. She heard footsteps.

"A little lost?"

Naomi didn't look up at Natasha. "You could say so. How did you know I was here?"

"David saw you come down," Natasha leaned against a dresser. "When you didn't resurface right away he found me."

"Worried about me?"

"Or about his job security in case you decide to do something drastic."

Naomi wished she could crack a smile but she remained only a few breaths away from hyperventilating.

"So you wanna tell me what this is about?"

"Wouldn't know where to start."

And that was the truth. What was in that box, even Natasha didn't know the full extent of.

"Would I be correct in guessing it has something to do with Jordan?"

Naomi nodded.

"And that box?"

Naomi nodded.

Natasha sighed. "You want to show him the journals."

Naomi finally looked up at her best friend. The concern in her eyes confirmed exactly how serious this was.

"Nay...you sure that's a good idea? I mean, you've never even showed me the journals and we've been friends since the sixth grade."

"He said he doesn't know me," Naomi eyes fell back to the locked chest. "Everything in there...that's me. The whole me."

"That's a part of you," Natasha corrected. "A part of your past to be exact. It's not who you are."

"But it's the part of me that he doesn't know," Naomi stood. "And he deserves to know. Even if we never end up together, for all the years that we were, he deserves to understand."

"Then just tell him." Natasha grabbed her hands. "I'm sure if you sit down and talk to him face to face..."

"No!" Naomi shook her head. Talk to Jordan? Tell him what had happened all those years she had been with Garth? What she had done? She couldn't even tell Ilana. That's where the journals had come from in the first place. It had been Ilana's idea to write it down and that's how Naomi had told her the whole story. But saying the words out loud...

Cold sliced through her. She began to tremble.

"Okay, okay," Natasha eased her back onto the crate and pulled up another one to sit down beside her. "I get it. Talking about it is not an option right now. But you will have to one day, Naomi."

Naomi knew that. But today would not be that day.

They both looked over at the box that held more secrets than anyone should have. Natasha held Naomi's hand.

"You can do this girl. If you could hustle your way into Carmelo Anthony's limo for an interview at the ESPYs without getting a beat down from La-La, you can show Jordan some journals."

Naomi smiled in spite of herself. What would she do without Natasha?

"Okay," Naomi got up and stepped forward. "Let's do this."

Chapter Twenty-two

The bat cracked against the ball, and sent it soaring. The hitter for the Yankees took off. He rounded first, second, third base and was about to go in for home plate. The fielders for Pittsburgh still chased the ball, which by all accounts was about to fall outside of their reach. It was a sure homerun for the Yankees. The crowd was on their feet. They went wild. Jordan sat in his field seat at Yankee Stadium, his feet propped up on the seat in front of him. The New York Yankees were his team. These were his season ticket seats after all. But he couldn't muster the energy to get up and cheer. He had lost his excitement. He had lost his drive.

Correction. Naomi had taken his drive and left him like this.

He looked down at the half bag of popcorn sitting on his chest and popped a few cold kernels into his mouth.

"Man, did you see that!" Malcolm yelled, still on his feet with the rest of the stadium. "That was amazing!"

"Yeah," Jordan murmured. He popped a few more kernels in his mouth. They tasted like cardboard.

Malcolm scowled and dropped back into his seat beside Jordan. It was the seat Naomi usually sat in. Although, she did very little sitting when they would come to games together. She had a loud mouth on her, and she would cheer with the best of them. She usually made friends with those in their section. She was half the entertainment of going to a ball game.

But there would be no more of that. No more of

Naomi, his red haired beauty.

"You know, if you're this miserable, you might as well get back with her," Malcolm said. "Forgive her for whatever happened in Trinidad already and move on. Cause this right here? This is pathetic."

"Shut up man," Jordan warned. "You don't know what it's like."

"Yeah, you're right, I don't," Malcolm wrinkled his nose. "And if this is what love looks like, I'd rather not. Have you even shaved in the last week?"

"I'm fine," Jordan rubbed a hand across his prickly jaw. "I look fine."

"About as fine as a grizzly," Malcolm mumbled. "About as friendly too."

"Man, what do you expect? The woman I was about to spend my life with betrayed me. Turned out to be something she wasn't."

"It is not that deep," Malcolm said. "So she was married before. Big freakin' deal. She wasn't married when she met you. It was a youthful indiscretion. Who hasn't had one or ten of those? And with the whole Trinidad thing, all she did was take care of her family the best way she knows how. At least you can be sure that when she's committed to you, she's in it for the long haul."

Jordan looked over at Malcolm, eyebrow raised. "Are you actually defending her?"

"Listen man, I have dealt with more than my fair share of women in my thirty-six years. And if Naomi's problems were the biggest problems any of them had, I would be married by now," Malcolm said.

"How am I supposed to trust her again?"

"With time," Malcolm said. "Who the heck told you it

was going to be easy? You love her, but its gotta be about more than the feeling. You have to be willing to love her past her flaws. So she messed up with this. Show her that it's okay to make mistakes; that you will still love her in spite of them. Cause if you start tripping over every mistake, all that's going to happen is that it's going to make her think twice about coming clean with you when other things happen."

"So, you're seriously suggesting I get back into things with her," Jordan said incredulously.

"I don't see that you have much of a choice," Malcolm said. "Her little hot body friend has been shaking her assets in your face since the moment you and Naomi split but you haven't even given her a second look. You're clearly not interested in being with anyone else. Naomi has your heart on a chain around her neck. You might as well be where your vital organs are."

Jordan scowled but said nothing. He sunk low in his chair and took a long gulp from his soda. Malcolm was right. Five weeks had passed but he hadn't stopped thinking about Naomi. He just couldn't get past the fact that she had lied to him. What else was she hiding? How many more secrets were waiting in her past to come out and bite him? He might miss her like cray, but he wasn't ready to put himself back into that chaos yet.

"What?"

"I thought you were going to try and work things out," Malcolm said.

"It's not that simple, man," Jordan shook his head. "I can't just pretend like nothing happened. I need more time to think this through."

Malcolm nodded. "You're right. And a noisy baseball stadium is not the place to do it."

Jordan's eyes widened. "Excuse me?"

"You have gots to go, bruh," Malcolm said dryly. "You're killing my baseball buzz."

"You're kicking me out of my season ticket seats?"

Malcolm shrugged. "It's not like you're actually paying attention to the game."

Jordan opened his mouth to argue but closed it. Malcolm was right. His head was definitely not in the game. And truthfully, this was the last place he wanted to be. At least if he was home he could try and get some work done.

Jordan got up and grabbed his jacket. "You're right man. I'm outta here."

Malcolm gave him a short wave. "Peace!"

Peace. Jordan shook his head. That was exactly what he needed but it seemed a long way coming. As he suffered through traffic back to Manhattan, he could not help but think back over the four years he had known Naomi. No matter how he tried, he could not get past the image of the smart, beautiful, interesting woman he had come to fall in love with. He had always known that there were layers upon layers of Naomi that he had not scratched the surface of. Jordan had looked forward to spending the rest of his life pulling them back and getting to the heart of her. Now the unknown of her scared him.

The thoughts continued to twist around in his mind as he shut off the car in his underground parking spot and headed up to the main floor of his condo building. A quick stop at his mailbox revealed that he had a lot to catch up on. As he took the elevator up, Jordan sifted through the piles of personal bills as well as business documents and invoices that he sometimes had sent to his home. He stepped off the elevator onto his floor and had just reached the bottom of the mail pile when he came across the padded envelope.

He stopped dead in the middle of his ninth floor hallway

as he stared at the return address. It was from Street Life, from Naomi.

Part of him wanted to send it back without opening it. The other part wanted to drop everything and rip into it right away. It had been five weeks, two days and seven hours since he had last seen Naomi. Since he had walked out of her niece's hospital room in Port of Spain and out of her life. But every bit of him ached for her. When Amanda gave him the engagement ring Naomi had returned to him through her, he had stormed out of the room in anger, partly because Naomi had returned the ring, and partly because she had done it through his sister and robbed him of the chance to see her. He should have been glad. He had been the one to call the whole thing off. At least he could take it back to the jeweler and get part of his money back. But he had been too much of a coward to take the ring back. Instead it sat in a corner of his sock drawer, feeding a hopeless dream that it might someday end up back on the finger of its original owner. And here he was, standing in the hallway, hoping that something in this envelope might undo all the wrong that had happened between him and Naomi.

But life didn't work like that. There was too much to be undone. It would take more than a padded envelope to change that.

Jordan dug his keys out of his pocket and let himself into his condo. He dropped the mail on the side table and kicked off his shoes. He almost made it to the kitchen. But his curiosity and his hope pulled him back like an invisible cord. The rest of the mail scattered to the ground as he pulled out Naomi's envelope and ripped it open. Inside were two faded clothbound notebooks held together with a well worn rubber band. He pulled out the note tucked in the front. He ran his fingers over her name, embossed on the top and realized just how pathetic he was before he began to read.

Jordan:

You were right. I did not give you a chance to know me. I was wrong for that. But maybe I can make it up right now. I don't know what will happen with us, but whatever happens, I hope you can forgive me for hurting you. Despite what you might think, the real me loves the real you.

Forever yours,

Naomi

Sliding the rubber band off the notebooks, Jordan opened the first one and started reading. An hour later, he still hadn't moved.

Chapter Twenty-three

"Knock, Knock!"

"Come in," Jordan called without looking up from the sheet of paper in front of him.

Kim slipped through the office door and laid a stack of documents on his growing to-do pile. "I have a few things to confirm befo- "

She stopped when Jordan held up a finger for her to wait as he scribbled. She smiled and sat down in a chair across from his desk and waited.

It hadn't been the first time he had kept her waiting. In fact, in the past couple of weeks, it had almost become a common occurrence. But the mail pick-up was at one p.m. and he wanted to make sure this particular note was in it when it came. Tomorrow would be too late.

There was no hesitation in his words as he wrote. Not like the first time he penned a note, after he had finished the first two journals. Jordan still got a chill every time he thought about the night that he stood at his front door and read the first two of Naomi's journals. They had shocked him to the core, so much so, that he needed to take the following day off from work just to regroup.

It was almost as if he read about a stranger. The woman who had dealt with the mistreatment that Naomi had written about seemed miles away from the woman who had been by his side for the past few years. At first, he was confused about why she would ever hide the truth about what she had gone through with Garth from him. It would have explained so much - including why she had been so hesitant to commit to their relationship back when they first started dating. But the more he read, the more he knew that was exactly why she hadn't shared it. She had spent so long putting on a show for others, keeping her thoughts and feelings to herself, that even when she wanted to, she didn't know how to share them with someone else.

But she had found a way to share it with him. And that glimmer of hope that had remained buried so deep in his heart began to shine through the darkness of his hurt and disappointment in tiny but visible rays.

"You know if you want, I can always come back..." Kim offered.

"Nope." Jordan folded the note and stuffed it into a blue envelope from the stack in his drawer. "I'm done. Can you..."

Kim smiled knowingly and took the sealed envelope from him. "Of course."

Jordan grinned. "Okay, what do you have for me?"

"Henry from Starwood called. They want you to submit an RFP for their new Bahamas project; the building owners sent over a new contract for another five year lease on our offices; Ron called to confirm that the Thirty Under Thirty board can still use our meeting room next week and Jeff wants to know if you will be a plus one for his anniversary party."

Jordan shook his head. What Jeff really wanted to know was, what the situation was with him and Naomi.

"Pull up the request for proposal we did for that Sheraton hotel in Hawaii and start modifying it based on the info we have about the Bahamas project; Jeff and I will discuss the lease at our meeting tomorrow morning and get back to the owners by the end of the week; and please call Ron and tell him the meeting is a go."

Kim nodded as she wrote. "And the anniversary party?"

Jordan rubbed a hand over his face. Plus one versus going solo. A place to grab a late dinner when he found himself at work after hours. Company on a Saturday night. These were the things that had become issues for him since he and Naomi split. Funny the way your life changed when you found yourself suddenly single after four years. It wasn't like there weren't women he could go out with. There just weren't any that he wanted to go out with.

"Tell Jeff I'll get back to him."

"How about you get back to me now?"

The booming voice caught both Jordan and Kim's attention. They looked up. Kim hid a smile as she rose from her chair and slipped past Jeff to exit the office. Jordan stared at the tall wide-shouldered man, who still carried the linebacker frame that had served him well in his three years in the NFL. He dropped his two hundred and twenty pounds into the seat Kim had vacated and squinted at Jordan.

"What's with the stalling, Lennox? I know Candy dropped off that invitation about two months ago. She's chewing my ear off about your RSVP."

Only because Naomi probably hadn't returned any of Candy's calls. It was amazing how many relationships were affected when two people parted ways.

Jordan leaned back in his chair. "A lot has changed in two months. But you can go ahead and tell Candy I'll be flying solo."

Jeff scowled. "So you telling me you and Naomi won't be making it to the end zone?"

Jordan shifted uncomfortably in his chair. Not because of Jeff's scowl - that he had become used to in the two decades he had known the man. He didn't know how to answer the question. The truth was when it came to Naomi, he didn't know the answers to anything. One moment he was optimistic about them, the next moment he felt like it was a lost cause.

"So what is this, the twenty-fifth anniversary?" Jordan dodged his business partner's question. "Feels like you and Candy have been married forever."

Jeff grunted. "Some days it feels like forever."

"But it's gotta be worth it," Jordan said thoughtfully. "I mean, you guys got married almost right out of high school, survived your NFL career and three kids...seems like a miracle."

"Not a miracle, Lennox," Jeff said. "Just hard work. Something I find you young bucks aren't willing to put in nowadays when it comes to a relationship."

Jordan took his friend's crack at him head on without flinching. It was easy for Jeff to judge him. He didn't know what Naomi had done. Or rather - what she hadn't told him she had done. And as much as her past explained a lot of it, it didn't excuse her hiding it from him.

"Did you ever feel like..." Jordan slowly spun his chair sideways and glanced out the window. "Like chucking the whole thing?"

"You mean did I ever feel like leaving my wife?" Jeff asked bluntly. "Of course I have. Candy may be cute and sweet, but she can be a pain in the butt when she wants to be. And there are times when she's driven me straight up the wall. I've had to walk out of my own house to keep myself from ending up in handcuffs. But I always came back. I stood before God and committed to be with her until one of us kicked the bucket and I don't mess with God."

Jeff cracked the slightest smile. "Besides, she may be crazy, but she's my crazy woman and I love her. I'll fight the whole world before I let anyone hurt her."

Jordan shook his head. "You guys don't look like you ever fight."

"Don't be fooled," Jeff said with a raised eyebrow. "We get into it sometimes. She does stupid stuff, but so do I. We're just willing to work through it, that's all."

"But aren't there some things that are too much for any relationship to handle?"

"Maybe," Jeff said. "But my willingness to forgive hasn't encountered any yet."

Jordan squeezed the bridge of his nose.

Jeff sat forward. "Look Lennox, if you want me to tell you that it's gonna be easy, I can't. If you think Naomi did you dirty and it's too bad for you to forgive her, then do what you have to do. But if you think you're gonna find a woman who's not gonna bring you something you have to forgive her for then you're fooling yourself. Nobody's perfect. And if she looks perfect, then she's lying. But if she's showed you who she is then at least you know what you're getting into, and you'll know how to love her."

"Why does it have to be this hard?" Jordan asked.

"If it were easy, would it really be worth it?"

Jeff stood without waiting for Jordan's answer. "I'll give Candy your answer. And by the way, you should get some rest. You look like crap."

Jordan didn't need a mirror to confirm that Jeff was right. With the number of sleepless nights he'd had in the past few weeks, he knew the bags under his eyes were large enough to store his winter wardrobe. No matter how much he thought breaking his engagement with Naomi had been the right thing to do, he still didn't feel at ease. In his heart, he had forgiven Naomi and was still in love with her. But in his mind, he wasn't sure he could trust her again.

He put his head back and closed his eyes. He needed some peace. And the only way that was going to happen was if he got both his heart and his mind to be in the same place. If only that were an easy thing to do. But the truth was, nothing looked easy anymore.

Chapter Twenty-Four

"He's here!"

Naomi scrambled away from the window where she had been watching for the postman and ran out her office towards the stairs.

"Geez, Naomi, slow down! You are going to break your neck on those stairs."

Despite Natasha's caution, Naomi continued her trot down the stairs, but managed to keep her pace to a brisk walk through the office to the entrance instead of a run like she wanted to. She got there just in time for the elevator doors to open.

"Ms. Savoy..."

"Hey Harold. How's it going? Those for us?" Naomi asked reaching for the bundle of mail in his hands.

The balding gentleman smirked as he released the mail to her. "Expecting something?"

Naomi shrugged as she distractedly flipped through the pile. "What makes you think that?"

"I don't know," Natasha said dryly. "Maybe your lack of manners."

Naomi's head popped up guilty. "Sorry, Harold."

He chuckled. "No worries." He stepped back into the elevator. "You might want to check the blue one at the back first though."

Naomi grinned and skipped to the back where sure enough there was a light blue envelope with her name handwritten on the front. She held the envelope to her nose briefly. When she caught the slight scent of sandalwood, her eyes drifted closed.

"Wow," Natasha folded her arms. "You're a hot mess."

Naomi smiled. "Don't question what you don't understand, Tash."

She shoved the rest of the mail at Natasha then pushed through the nearest door into the copy room - or rather copy closet - since the space was barely large enough for the commercial photocopier and shelves of office supplies it held.

"What I don't understand is why Jordan can't send mail to your house instead of to the office," Natasha grabbed the door before it closed and squeezed inside the tiny room.

"Please," Naomi pursed her lips. "Sending mail to my apartment is like taking a walk through Brooklyn at night. You never know what might happen, but chances are it won't be good. Since I moved to that place, all my mail's been coming here. I'm pretty much here all the time anyway."

Natasha nodded. "Good point."

The door slid closed behind Natasha leaving the women with less than two feet of space between them.

"Do you mind?" Naomi nodded towards the door.

"Uh, you bet I do." Natasha folded her arms and leaned against the door. "You didn't make me watch for the mail man for half an hour for nothing. "

Naomi pretended to pout. "This is private."

Natasha pursed her lips. "It wasn't private two weeks ago when you begged me to read his first note because you were too scared to know what he said. Now when it starts getting juicy you want to cut a sister out? I don't think so."

Naomi rolled her eyes. But she couldn't deny Natasha's claim. When the first note from Jordan had arrived a week after she sent him the journals, Naomi nearly had a breakdown in her office. She had seen his scrawly handwriting and caught a whiff of his usual scent on the envelope and immediately summoned Natasha. If her friend hadn't opened the note and assured her it wouldn't break her heart, it probably would still be sitting on her desk.

That first note had only been two words, *Thank you*. She had taken that as a good sign and sent him the rest of the journals. His next note back had been a little longer and she couldn't help but respond in kind. Pretty soon the letters flew back and forth between them, occasionally overlapping in the mail and going faster than probably the US Postal service could keep up with. Now, Naomi's favorite part of the day was the arrival of the postman. She had not seen Jordan or exchanged a phone call, email or text message with him in close to two months, but it felt like he was with her every day. And she missed him now more than ever.

"Okay fine, you can stay." Naomi pulled herself up on the narrow worktable that was pushed up against the wall. "But you're not reading this one."

Natasha snorted. "That's what you think."

Naomi was too engrossed in the letter to respond.

Dear Red,

As I am writing this, your letters sit on my desk in a pile. Every now and then I take them out and read through them again. Then they are tucked away safely beside the journals that you have shared with me. Together they make up the missing pieces of the puzzle of you that I have longed to know. I feel like I have learned more about you in these past couple of weeks than I have in the four years we have been together. And instead of scaring me away, it makes me love you more. Makes me long to hold you. Makes me think about the feel of your soft skin. The smell of your hair first thing in the

*morning when it's still wet. The delicious taste of your lips after
you've been drinking that berry hibiscus thing from Starbucks that
you love. And sometimes when I'm lying in bed at night and
thinking about the fact that you should be beside me now as my wife
and lover, I have a hard time falling asleep. Go take a moment to
catch your breath as you think about that.*

Naomi closed her eyes and laid her head back against the
wall. She willed the gallop of her heart to slow down to a
normal pace. Jordan was killing her softly, and he wasn't
even in the room. Boy, did she miss him.

*You're back with me? Good. Cause here's where it gets serious. I'm
glad that you can finally be open with me like this, but if there's any
possibility for us, we have to be able to be this honest with each other
all the time. In person, face to face, every day, every moment. Can
you do that, Red? Can we face the ugliness in our past and present
head on together? Can we trust that God and the love we have for
each other will keep us together? I'm willing. Are you?*

Still yours,

Jordan

Naomi closed her eyes and held the letter to her chest.

"Was it that bad?" Natasha almost whispered.

Naomi wiped at the tears that streamed down her face.
She opened her eyes.

"No," she shook her head. "It was that good. Things
might not be so hopeless after all."

Natasha smiled slowly before nodding. "Does this mean
you guys are getting back together?"

Naomi slid off the table and tucked the letter back into
the envelope. "I wouldn't go that far."

She wouldn't dare be so presumptuous in her hope. But
at least there was hope. And it was brighter today than it had
been for a long time.

Before either of them could say another word, there were two knocks and then the door opened.

"If you guys are done hanging out in the copy room, Naomi, your three-thirty is here," David said with a smirk.

Natasha set her hands on her hips, and almost poked Naomi in the stomach in the process. "Boy, I sign your paychecks. I will hang out in the copy room all dang day if I want."

His eyes widened as his mouth opened and closed. "I was just...I'm sorry...I...uh..."

Naomi rolled her eyes and squeezed past Natasha. "Don't mind her, David. Show my guest to my office. I'll be right there."

"Ok." He hurried off, his eyes glued to the floor.

Naomi turned around and glared at Natasha who cackled behind her. "Behave."

"Hey, you gotta put a little fear into their behinds sometimes," Natasha grinned as they headed back to their offices. "Keeps them off balance, and you in control."

If keeping someone off balance was the key to staying in control, then Jordan had all the power right then, because Naomi's head still spun from his letter. She wanted time to read it again in private and think about it some more but by the time she got to her office, a plump stylishly dressed young woman sat in front of her desk waiting.

"Hi, I'm Naomi Savoy," she reached out her hand to the young woman. "Sorry for keeping you waiting."

"Oh, it's no trouble at all," the woman hopped to her feet and grasped Naomi's hand. "I'm Teresa Jones. I'm so glad you could fit me in."

"It's my pleasure," Naomi said honestly as she directed Teresa over to a small sitting area near the corner of her office. "With all that the Thirty Under Thirty Committee has done to help me, I am always willing to help out other up and coming young entrepreneurs. Can I get you anything? Water? Tea?"

"Water would be great, thanks," Teresa took a seat in an armchair in front of a small table. Naomi grabbed two water bottles from the concealed mini-fridge near her desk and took a seat across from the young woman.

"So you've been nominated for the Woman of Courage Award," Naomi began after they had both taken a sip of their beverages. "Congratulations."

"Oh, thank you so much," Teresa said enthusiastically. "When they called me and told me, I was so excited. You know, even if I don't win, I am just so glad to be acknowledged and to get to work with people like you. When Mr. Lennox told me I would be mentored by the founder of Street Life Magazine, I couldn't believe it."

Naomi blinked. "Jordan Lennox? He's the one who directed you to me?"

"Oh yes," Teresa nodded. "When he heard my story he said he thought we would be a good match and that we could probably learn a lot from each other. Although to be honest, I don't know what someone as accomplished as you could learn from me, though I know I will definitely learn a lot from you."

Naomi was glad the woman continued to talk. It gave her a chance to catch her breath at the mention of Jordan. She was still a little off kilter from earlier.

"Well, if Mr. Lennox says that we can learn from each other, we likely will," Naomi said with a smile. "I have found that he is not often wrong. So, tell me about your business."

If Naomi thought Teresa was chatty before, the woman became even more garrulous when the topic of her business came up.

"My business is called Sincerely Yours," Teresa said as her eyes brightened. "It's a specialty gift service where you can order customized gift sets for any occasion."

According to Teresa, her business started three years earlier with her making gift baskets for friends and family members on request. When she did the wedding favors for a friend's wedding, she began to get requests from other people to do gift baskets and party favors for various events. Pretty soon, she ran a full fledged business out of the basement of her home.

"That's amazing, Teresa," Naomi said genuinely impressed. "So how have your sales been?"

"Well at first, I didn't check often to see how much I spent versus how much I charged for the baskets," Teresa said. "When the orders began to increase, I started to get more serious about that and adjusted my prices. I still struggle with that."

"Well, we can definitely help you there," Naomi said. "We can set up a pricing model that works for you, that you can apply across the board with all your products. We can also talk about how you can do some more marketing to increase your sales. That is if you can handle more clients."

"Oh yes, I would love that," Teresa said. "I have someone I call in to help me when I have big event orders or during high demand seasons like Christmas and Mother's Day."

Teresa looked thoughtful. "I would actually love to be able to have her work with me full time. She is such a faithful employee. But I worry that I will not always have enough business to sustain her employment."

Naomi nodded. "I definitely know what that's like. Having employees, people who depend on you, adds a whole dimension to the business-owner model. I can't tell you how many sleepless nights I used to have. I worried about whether or not business would keep up enough for me to sustain all my employees. But I think with a little work, you can have a booming business, Teresa. You might even need two employees!"

Teresa smiled. "You know about a year into my business, things were doing really well. I got a lot of orders for special events. I even had my website up and took orders through there. I was ready to expand. But then I had a few...challenges...and I had to shut down for a while."

Naomi noticed the pained expression that briefly graced Teresa's face when she mentioned having challenges.

"But now, I have my website back online and at least I have a way for people to always contact me," Teresa said. "God has been so good to me. He has blessed me so much to bring me to this point."

Naomi nodded. "Is your faith important to you?"

"Oh yes," Teresa said. "It is the center of my life. You know, life has been a challenge for me as a single mother. And even before that. If it wasn't for God's mercy... I don't know how I would have made it."

Teresa's voice trailed off as her eyes went moist. She dug into her purse for a tissue. Without thinking, Naomi reached over and grabbed the woman's hand. With her other hand, she grabbed a box of tissues off the side table and offered them to her.

"Thank you," Teresa said when she managed to pull herself together. "I'm sorry I got so emotional. I am not usually like this. But talking about Sincerely Yours and about my faith has made me think about everything I have had to go through to get here."

"I know it must have been hard for you starting a

business while taking care of your child on your own," Naomi said gently. "I was single and had the support of my family and friends when I started Street Life Magazine and even then it was a struggle. There were days when I would just come home and cry because I didn't think I would be able to make it. I can imagine this has been even more true for you."

"Oh, much more than you know," Teresa said. "It wasn't just the stress of taking care of my son and starting a business. There was so much more."

She looked at Naomi a long time before taking a deep breath. "Like I told you, I started my business three years ago. At the time, I was living with my son's father. We were supposed to get married but it never happened. But at least I had someone who loved me. Or I thought he loved me. I convinced myself he did, which is why I forgave him after he hit me the first time."

Naomi sucked in a sharp breath.

"He told me he was sorry," Teresa stared at the wall behind Naomi's head. "Told me it was a mistake. It would never happen again. But it did. Over and over. One time I tried to leave. But he found me at my mother's house and convinced her that he loved me. She let him take me back to his home."

Tears pooled in the woman's eyes, but never fell as she continued. "You know, once he hit me so hard that two of my teeth fell out. I have partial dentures now because of it. But I stayed because I thought, if I loved him more, if I was a better fiancée, he would be better. And sometimes it worked. But he never changed. And I never changed, until the day I ended up in the hospital with a broken arm. That's when I had to stop my business because I couldn't work with a broken arm and I was too ashamed to ask for help because then I would have had to explain what happened. There was some good from it though. While I was in the hospital, I found out I was pregnant. And that changed everything. It wasn't about me anymore. It was about my baby, this life inside of me. And I knew I would never let him touch me again."

Teresa said that her fiancé was in jail now. But Naomi barely heard it. Something inside her had shut down. She couldn't speak. Couldn't think. She was Teresa. It was as if this woman had told her life to her. She heard it and saw it out loud for the first time.

"Oh Miss Savoy! I am so sorry," Teresa reached across and grabbed Naomi's hand. "I did not mean to make you cry. I am okay now. My son is okay now. It's okay."

Naomi shook her head. No, it wasn't okay. She didn't know how long she sat there. Teresa offered to call someone for her but Naomi shook her head. She just needed a moment. She closed her eyes and counted backwards from ten and reminded herself that she was safe. Then she took a deep breath and opened her eyes. Teresa stared at her as if she had sprouted a second head. Naomi knew the woman must have been wondering what kind of psycho Jordan had sent her to.

She sighed, released the breath she had taken. "I think I know why Mr. Lennox sent you to me."

Then she told Teresa her story, of her marriage to Garth, of what it had been like living with him. She didn't tell her everything - there were still many things too painful to talk about. But she shared with that virtual stranger more than she had ever been able to talk about before. And when she was done, she was surprised to find herself not in pieces on the floor.

"You don't talk about this with anyone, do you?" Teresa asked knowingly.

Naomi shook her head.

"I can tell." Teresa nodded. "Because you look down when you speak, like you are afraid, like the words will hurt you if you speak them out loud. But let me tell you, they only hurt you when you keep them inside. When you let them out, when you tell people your story, then it loses its power over you."

Naomi looked up at Teresa as if she was crazy.

The woman laughed. "I know. I was like you too. But I found, the more I shared my story, the less afraid I was to talk about it. The less painful it was. The less powerful it was. The stronger and freer I felt. "

"I don't know if I can," Naomi shook her head. "You know, I have so many people in my life who love me: my mother, my brother, my best friend, a man who wanted to marry me. But it's so hard to tell them this. To say the words...I am so..."

"Afraid?" Teresa asked. "There is no fear in love, my friend. Perfect love casts out all fear."

That was what Ilana had told her. That's what God had whispered to her. She still had to remind herself to believe it.

"This thing, the abuse, it is like a secret," Teresa's eyes glowed with wisdom as she spoke. "The fewer people who know it, the more power it has. But once it is out there, once you tell it, it has no more power over you. No one can use it against you. It is like you release it, and all the pain that comes with it."

Naomi couldn't help but smile as she watched the light radiate from Teresa's face. It was a light of joy. Of peace. Real peace. The kind that came from God and the healing that He gave. Naomi wanted that. And it shocked her to know that God had been waiting to give that to her all along, if she would only claim it. Teresa had reminded her of that.

"You know what, Teresa," Naomi said. "You came here

for me to mentor you, but I think you just mentored me in a way you could never understand."

Teresa grinned. "Guess Mr. Lennox was right after all."

Naomi sighed. "Like I said, he usually is."

Chapter Twenty-five

"So you're really going to this thing aren't you?"

Naomi looked back at Camille who was sprawled out on her bed with a bag of chips.

"No smarty, I just sat down for two hours and let you straighten my hair for fun," Naomi said dryly.

"Alright, alright," Camille popped a potato chip into her mouth. "You ain't gotta get all crusty with me. I'm just saying, if you're trying to get your man back, you could at least buy yourself a new dress. Something short, tight and low cut in the front and back."

Naomi rolled her eyes and turned back to the mirror where she applied her eye shadow. "I am not twenty-one anymore. I'll leave that over-sexy-stripper look to you and your friends."

"Shut up," Camille laughed and tossed a chip at Naomi. Naomi grinned. It was nice having Camille back. Having her around. She realized that in the past few months she hadn't spent nearly enough time with her, just hanging out enjoying her niece's company. All that would change. Regardless of what did or did not happen with Jordan, she would make sure Camille never got sidelined again.

"Any plans for tonight?" Naomi asked.

Camille's face fell. "Nay..."

"I'm not prying, just making conversation," Naomi kept her gaze on the mirror.

Camille eyed her suspiciously as she munched on the chips. "Crystal is coming over. I'm gonna put in some box braids for her."

Naomi turned around and frowned at her niece. "She better be paying you for that."

"No doubt," Camille said. "Ain't no free labor happenin' up in here."

Naomi smiled. "Good. I don't want anyone taking advantage of my niece."

"Naomi?"

"Hmm?"

Camille took so long to answer that Naomi almost put down the mascara brush to look back at her.

"Thanks," she finally said. "For everything."

Naomi blinked back tears, but kept her voice steady as she continued to work on her eyelashes.

"That's what family is for, hun." She capped her mascara and reached for the lipstick. "Now, go get my dress out of the closet so you can help me into it. My ride will be here in about fifteen minutes."

Camille scrambled off the bed and ran to the closet. Naomi was sure she would take the opportunity to rifle through it for anything near her size. By the time Naomi got back, she would surely be missing a few items.

"Ooh, Nay-Nay, this dress is off the hook!" Camille squealed as she rushed back into the room with the hanger. "You're going to have Jordan panting like a dog."

Naomi laughed nervously. "I sure hope so."

The time seemed to fly and before Naomi knew it, her ride waited for her downstairs.

"There's leftovers in the fridge but if you want to order something, there's money and menus in the kitchen drawer," Naomi grabbed her purse and headed towards the door.

"Naomi, wait!"

Naomi turned around, her dress swung as Camille hurried towards her with a bottle of what looked like body spray.

"Hold out your arms."

"I already have on perfume," Naomi protested.

"This is not perfume," Camille grabbed her aunt's left arm and misted it with the liquid.

Naomi squealed when the light began to shimmer and reflect off her skin. "Are you covering me with glitter! What do you think I am? Sixteen?"

Camille rolled her eyes, and spread the liquid over Naomi's arm like lotion. "It is not glitter, but it will make your skin glow. Jordan's going to think you're an angel."

"Yeah, an angel from some kid's kindergarten class drawing."

"Oh! Be quiet," Camille grabbed Naomi's right arm and sprayed before Naomi could stop her.

"I can't believe I am letting you do this to me..."

"Turn around!" Camille ordered. She prayed Naomi's exposed back and then before she could stop her rubbed a bit on her chest where the top of her dress dipped very slightly towards her cleavage.

"Okay enough!" Naomi pulled the door open. "Bye!"

"Have fun!"

Naomi hurried down the stairs and out into the cool night air. She paused when she saw the limo parked in front of her building.

"Really, Amanda?" Naomi asked when the door opened

and the woman peeked her head out. "Limousine?"

"Well, you know me," Amanda waved Naomi inside. "Go big or go home."

Naomi rolled her eyes as she slipped into the back seat and closed the door behind her.

Amanda winked. "Love the dress by the way."

"Oh, this old thing?" Naomi said with a grin. "It was just something I had lying around."

Amanda laughed. "I'm sure."

"So do I know any of the recipients this year?" Naomi asked as she settled back into her seat across from Amanda's.

"No, but next year, I hope you will," Amanda folded her hands in her lap as sat back. "Have you ever thought about being a part of the committee for the Thirty under Thirty awards?"

Naomi blinked, not sure if Amanda was being serious. "No."

"Well, you should." Amanda said earnestly. "You've recommended individuals for the award almost every year since you received it. Many of them have gone on to do really well with the money they've received. We have a couple of people retiring this year and I think you have an eye for young talent. You'd be great on the committee."

Naomi bit her lip thoughtfully. Her life was already over scheduled as it was, but the thought of encouraging and building young entrepreneurs excited her. Working with Teresa on expanding her business had energized her more than anything she had done career wise recently. She could definitely see herself getting more involved.

"Maybe," Naomi said. "I would have to think about it."

"Well, start thinking," Amanda said. "Because I plan to

recommend you at our board meeting next week."

Naomi stared out the window and watched the New York lights pass them by. She knew she would enjoy working on the committee, but it would mean seeing Jordan pretty frequently as he was also a part of the team. As it stood, their lives didn't intersect that much, and that would be a good thing if it turned out that they didn't end up together. She wasn't sure if she could bear seeing him all the time, having him be that close but so emotionally far away.

"Don't worry about Jordan," Amanda said knowingly. "Regardless of what happens, he'll stay professional. It won't be a problem."

Naomi sighed and rested her hand on her cheek. That was easy for her to say.

Chapter Twenty-six

Jordan checked his watch, scanned the room, pulled at his necktie then checked his watch again. He retrieved a glass of water from a table nearby, took a sip then promptly discarded it. He checked his watch for a third time.

"Oh for heaven's sake, Jordan Isaiah Lennox, will you stop fidgeting! You are about to give me a nervous breakdown."

Jordan threw an apologetic glance towards the regal looking woman seated at the table with him.

"Sorry, mom." He sighed. "I guess I am a little on edge tonight. Where is Amanda? I thought she would be here by now."

"Your sister has never been on time a day in her life," Elizabeth Lennox said as she adjusted her place setting. "I don't know why you thought it would be different today."

"Well, she is a part of the Thirty under Thirty board," Jordan said, unable to keep the annoyance out of his voice. "You would think she could be on time for her own event."

Elizabeth chuckled and Jordan looked over at his mom.

"What?"

Elizabeth smiled. "Nothing my dear."

He narrowed his eyes at her suspiciously, but she just smiled and settled her attention on the printed event program. Unable to stay still a moment longer, he stood up suddenly and strode through the crowded ballroom to the men's room at the back. He was glad to find it empty and took the opportunity to splash some water on his face. He dried the damp spots with a paper towel then stared at himself in the mirror.

"Come on, Jordan. It's not that big a deal. You're just going to walk up to her and tell her how you feel. Lay it all out there and let the chips fall where they may. That's the plan. Just say how you feel."

He nodded at himself. He felt only marginally better after his pep talk. He headed towards the door.

"Say how you feel, say how you fee-."

The words died on his lips as his eyes caught a blaze of orange.

She was here.

Every beam of light in the room seemed to be attracted to her beautiful form as she smiled and greeted colleagues, awardees and fellow business persons. She was radiant. Her dress flowed gently over her curves then cascaded to the floor and glided around her like a haze of light. Her skin glowed like a warm summer sunset. Jordan longed to touch it, to feel its warmth.

He wavered between standing and watching her versus being closer to her, but eventually the tug of his emotions moved him across the room.

The band had started playing. Smooth jazz flowed through the ballroom and everyone seemed to move to the dance floor to take advantage of the opportunity to soak up everything the event had to offer. But he kept getting held up by people who knew him. She was mere steps away when his view was suddenly cut off by a broad figure.

"Jordan Lennox, it's good to see you."

"Judge Bryan," Jordan responded. He forced enthusiasm he didn't feel into his voice. "Good seeing you here."

"Yes well, I've heard a lot about these awards, but never

had the chance to attend until this year," the Judge said. "You guys are doing a great job, recognizing the young businessmen and women in this fine city."

Jordan nodded and tried to appear interested as the Judge went on, but he couldn't help but search for the flash of orange over the man's shoulder.

"Well, Judge, I'd love to stay and chat but..."

"Listen, Lennox," Judge Bryan put a hand on his shoulder before he could slip away. "Have you ever considered running for city council?"

"To be honest, sir, I haven't." In the corner of his eye, Jordan saw Naomi head towards the front of the room.

"Well, we've had an alderman position open up in the Bronx. With your family's history of success in city politics, I definitely think you should consider it."

"I'll keep it in mind," Jordan said. "Now, if you'll excuse me."

Jordan slipped away from the Judge before he could say another word and made a beeline for the front of the room to where Naomi stood near the stage. But before he could get near, the music faded and the lights went down on the room.

"Good evening everyone and welcome to New York City's 25th annual Thirty Under Thirty Awards."

There was a round of applause as all attention turned toward the stage and the chair of the committee, Ron Scarlett.

"This is very special evening for New York's young entrepreneurs."

Jordan searched the darkened room for Naomi. She was still by the stage. He whispered apologies as he discreetly tried to move towards her. He knew he could wait. She would likely be there all night. But if she wasn't, if she somehow left without him getting a chance to tell her how he felt, he wasn't sure he would be able to forgive himself.

He was so focused on getting to where she was that he barely heard what was going on. It wasn't until Naomi walked up the steps to the stage and the spotlight fell on her that he stood still.

"Good evening, everyone," Naomi said. "This evening, I am here to present the Woman of Courage award. This award is presented to a young woman who has had to overcome extraordinary odds in the pursuit of success. As a former recipient of this award, I was asked to say a little bit about what it means to be courageous."

Naomi paused. Jordan watched as emotion fluttered through her eyes, just before her gaze fell to the podium in front of her. He felt his chest tighten.

"But the truth is, I haven't been very courageous." She looked up and the pain in her eyes echoed in waves through him. "In fact, in many ways, I did not deserve this award when I received it several years ago. You see for a long time, I was a coward in my own life. I let a man who said he loved me hurt me over and over. Beat me until I couldn't recognize my own face in the mirror. Break me in ways that no woman should ever be broken. I allowed him to do this. And I let him make me believe it was my fault. I couldn't leave. I didn't have the courage to. But I thank God that he placed women of courage in my life. Women like my cousin, who saved me when I couldn't save myself. Women like my best friend, who caught me when I was about to fall again. Women like my mentor who helped me learn how to heal. Those were the real women of courage."

She lifted her chin and drew in a deep breath. "And as I listened to the stories of the four women nominated today, I recognized in them the courage that I found in the women who saved me. I know we only give one award, but all of them deserve to be up here today and so I invite to join me on stage: Estella Campbell, Juliet Johnson, Teresa Jones, and Kimone Keen.

There was a round of applause in the room and Jordan watched Teresa Jones wheel a beautifully dressed woman up the ramp to the stage. The other two women followed behind them. They were all familiar. He had met all the nominees and knew all of their stories personally. It had been a hard choice for the committee to choose just one. Naomi was right. They were all exceptional.

"And the recipient of this year's Woman of Courage award is…" Naomi paused to open the gilded envelope. "Juliet Johnson."

The slim, dark skinned woman stepped to the podium to the sound of more applause as she received the plaque and the envelope, which Jordan knew, held a sizeable check. Naomi hugged the woman tightly then hugged the other three nominees. She held on to Teresa a little longer than the rest.

"Thank you so much for this award," Juliet beamed at the crowd. "I am so grateful for this recognition and for all the support the committee has given to me and the other nominees. If there is one thing I have learned, it's that courage is not so much about overcoming the big things, but in getting up everyday and overcoming the doubts in yourself."

She turned to look back at Naomi. "And this woman here, though she thinks otherwise, has shown so much courage in her words today. This award is not just mine. It's Teresa's, Kimone's, Estella's and Naomi's too. So on behalf of all of us, thank you."

The applause, along with lots of cheers, sounded again as the five women left the stage together. Jordan wanted to add cheers to his applause but the lump in his throat kept him from speaking. It had lodged there after he heard Naomi. It was filled with pride, and with something he had never felt so strongly before as he did now - unconditional love.

Chapter Twenty-seven

Naomi's stride felt light as she walked down the steps of the stage with the other women ahead of her. Teresa had been right. Telling the truth about her past, taking it out of the realm of secrecy had loosened the chains it had over her. That moment, as she stared out at the hundreds of faces looking back at her, she had been terrified. The fear had almost paralyzed her. But the moment she let the words go, she felt freer than she had ever felt since everything had happened.

As she stepped off the last step, she wasn't surprised to see who was waiting for her. She hugged her friend tightly, remembered all the times when Natasha had held her up, because she was too much of a mess to hold up herself. There would never be enough words to express how much Naomi appreciated Natasha for those times.

"I am so proud of you, hun," Natasha said quietly.

Naomi pulled back and looked at her friend. "I don't say it enough, but thank you."

Natasha nodded and blinked rapidly. Naomi's eyes widened. "Oh my goodness, Natasha...are you...crying?"

"Shut up!" Natasha scowled. She swiped at her eyes and looked away. "I just have something in my eye. Probably one of your hairs. I barely had time to close my eyes when you pounced on me awhile ago."

Naomi grinned and folded her arms. "I pounced on you?"

"Yes," Natasha said as she dug through her purse for her compact. "For real, Naomi, you get way too emotional

175

sometimes."

"Do I?"

"You do." Natasha glared at her eyes in the mirror.

Naomi shook her head. "You need a tissue to get that hair out?"

"No, I'm fine." Natasha closed the compact and dropped it back into her purse.

"You sure? Cause your eyes look a little wet."

"That's just my new wet-look mascara," Natasha flipped her hair. "A lot of single men in here tonight. A girl's gotta pull out all the stops, you know what I'm saying?"

Naomi laughed and pulled her towards their table. "How about we let them finish handing out the awards before you start prowling?"

Natasha shook her head but let Naomi lead her away. "See, that was always your problem Naomi, you never remembered the importance of being ahead of the game."

They slipped into their seats even as the hosts announced the next set of awards. Naomi clapped at the appropriate times and tried to pay attention, but she couldn't stop her eyes from scanning the large dimly lit room.

Natasha leaned over. "You see him yet?"

"Who?" Naomi asked innocently.

"Oh, so we're gonna play that game?"

Naomi rolled her eyes. "No, I haven't seen him yet."

Natasha smiled and turned her eyes back to the stage. "Don't worry. He's here."

Naomi wasn't worried. At least she didn't think she was. But when the waiter had to refill her water glass three times before they had even finished presenting the awards, she knew she was fooling herself. When she stood up, Natasha glanced at her questioningly.

"Ladies' room," Naomi whispered.

Natasha looked at Naomi's empty glass. "I'll bet."

Naomi ignored her friend and walked down the side of the room quietly to the back and into the hallway where the washrooms were. She was glad to find them empty. After she handled her business, she stood in front of the mirror a moment and stared at the smile that seemed permanently fixed on her face. So much had happened in the past couple of weeks. It seemed like in the span of three months her whole life had changed. She had lost a few things, such as her fiancé, and the privacy around the secrets in her life. But she had also gained so much: a better relationship with her niece; the freedom to not be ashamed of her past, and the assurance that even if things didn't turn out perfectly, they would be okay. She would be okay. In the midst of it all, God had her back. And she would never lose that.

She took a deep breath then pushed through the door back into the hallway. Naomi had only taken two steps when something stopped her.

Sandalwood.

She turned around. There he was, leaned up against the wall, hands casually tucked in his pockets. He stared at her.

"Jordan."

"Red."

His name for her on his lips unlocked something warm and heady inside her. She remembered the first time he called her that. It had been their second date. They were supposed to go out for lunch but she had gotten caught in the rain and her normally straightened hair had reverted to its natural state. She hadn't had time to straighten it again before he showed up at her place so when he rung her doorbell, she answered the door with her hair a wild explosion of reddish-burgundy corkscrews on her head. Naomi hadn't known what to make of his open mouthed expression as he stared at her hair. But then he had reached out and gently tugged at one of her coils and grinned.

"Red, I like it," he had said. From then on, it became her signature hair color and she had been "Red" to him ever since.

"Hey."

In the background of her mind, she heard the distant sound of the hosts on stage and patters of applause, but all she could do was stare at Jordan. He wore a crisp Navy Armani suit that stretched across his broad frame as if tailor made for his immaculately toned body. The rich color of his burnt orange tie picked up the golden highlights in his skin. His head was clean shaven as always, but he had started growing in his moustache and beard and they were trimmed to sharp perfection. Naomi's stomach took a dive as she took in the whole picture.

Dear Lord, he was sexy.

Had it been that long that she had forgotten? Had eleven weeks erased the memory of how fine her man was? Her man. She couldn't shake it. She still thought of him that way - though she would never admit it to anyone but herself.

She didn't know how long they stood there and stared at each other, but there was no discomfort. No awkwardness. Even with everything that had happened between them over the past four years, it had never been awkward between them. Not even once.

"You look..." He shook his head in awe as his eyes roamed over her. "Stunning."

Heat crept up her neck and cheeks as he gazed at her. "Thanks."

"And by the way," He leaned off the wall and took a step towards her. "Congratulations."

Naomi tilted her head to the side and smiled. "I didn't win anything tonight."

He nodded. "You did. You just don't know it yet."

Naomi wanted to ask what he meant. But she was far too content to just stare at him, be this close to him, and enjoy the faintest scent of his cologne wrapped around her like a warm blanket. He reached out a hand. She took it without question. With fingers threaded together, they headed down the hallway away from the main gala hall towards the courtyard of Gustavinos.

The night air was cool. The outside quiet. Beautiful white lights twinkled through the foliage, setting the mood for a romantic evening. Or maybe that was just what Naomi hoped for and so she saw the romance in everything.

"I've been thinking about what you said," Naomi began as they walked slowly along the cobblestone path. "About me being open, being honest every moment with you."

She stopped walking and turned to look at him, expectancy in his eyes.

"I want to. I really do." she looked down. "But I've never done that before. With anyone." She looked up again. "I don't know how."

He took her other hand. "I know."

"And I don't want to disappoint you," she continued. "Because you have put up with so much from me already and you deserve so much better. I love you too much to hurt you again."

He tugged on their enjoined hands, pulled her closer toward him. "I know."

"But I'm afraid I might hurt you. Without meaning to.

Just because of who I am. There's so much about me you don't know." She closed her eyes for a moment. "So much I need to tell you, I need to say..."

He pulled her even closer, rested his forehead on hers. "Red, baby, I know."

Naomi sucked in a deep breath, kept her eyes closed. "So, how can you still want to be with me?"

He let go of her hands, placed his instead on the side of her neck. Jordan gently moved to cup her face.

"Because I love you," he whispered. "And that doesn't change because of what's in your past. I know this is hard for you, but I know the woman who stood on that stage tonight and told her story, the woman who bared her heart to me in those journals, the woman who fought to get her life back from that monster...that woman is going to fight to make us work."

She placed her hands outside his even as tears slid down her face. "But it shouldn't be that hard."

"If it were easy, it wouldn't be worth it," he murmured back.

Sobs broke her throat and he pulled her into him, buried her in his arms. Naomi wrapped her arms around him as she slipped her head into the place between his shoulder and neck that felt like home to her.

Why was God so good to her?

"I missed you so much," he murmured against her hair.

Naomi nodded, still too choked up on sobs for words. She was so lucky - so blessed for even the possibility of another chance with this man. When she could speak again, she pulled back to look up at him. She needed to see his face, his eyes, know that this was real.

"So, we're really doing this? You and me?"

He tucked a strand of her hair behind her ear. "As long as you're in it one hundred percent."

Naomi nodded. "I'm in."

"Now and the rest of our lives?"

Naomi smiled. "Now and the rest of our lives."

He nodded. "Good. In that case, there's something you need to have. Or should I say, have back."

He slipped his hand inside his jacket and returned with a white gold, seven carat diamond ring. Naomi's hands flew to her mouth.

"Recognize this?"

She nodded. Then she let him take her left hand and slip it back onto her ring finger. It felt like her world had been tumbling and shaking but now it had finally settled back into place.

"Jordan, are you sure?" She asked even as she stared at the ring. "I mean, I want this. I want this so bad. But maybe we need more time. We need to...know more...before we try and do this again."

Jordan nodded. "I agree. I'm not saying we're getting married tomorrow, or next week. Just think of it as a reservation for the future."

Naomi looked up into his eyes and shook her head. "You don't need a reservation." She tapped the left side of her chest. "Your spot is always right here."

He swept her into his arms. "Music to my ears."

Before she could even think of another word, she felt the sweet pressure of his lips on hers. And then every thought melted from her head. Every doubt and fear she had ever had about them went up like vapor. No matter what her past was, and no matter what her future held, she was sure that she would make it and this man - this utterly amazing man - would be right there beside her. He was hers, she was his and God was creating with them something new that was not just for a time or a season. This was something that would last now and for the rest of their lives.

About the Author

Rhonda Bowen knew she would be a writer as early as eighth grade when she wrote her first novel with a classmate in a dollar notebook. While waiting for the day to come she completed a degree in Communications and spent a few years working in Public Relations and Event Planning. Throughout this time however, her desire to write stayed alive. She eventually completed her first novel, *__Man Enough for Me__*, which was released under Kensington Books' Dafina imprint in February 2011.

Several years, a stint in Asia and a career change to youth work finds her still writing. She has written four romance novels and her books have been featured in PUBLISHERS WEEKLY and LIBRARY JOURNAL. When not writing or engaging her youth, she enjoys spending time with her family, trying on shoes she can't afford and enjoying the great outdoors. Visit her online at www.rhondabowen.com , www.facebook.com/RhondaBowenBooks or drop her a note at rhondakbowen@gmail.com.

Other books by Rhonda Bowen

Man Enough For Me
March 2011

Feisty and fabulous PR maven Jules Jackson has everything under control, which essentially means juggling two jobs, a difficult mother and all the drama of her crazy friends. But there's one area where she's sorely lacking: her love life. It feels like every time she's had a chance at romance, it's just been a test for her of how much she's willing to put up with. So she's just about given up on men when she meets Germaine Williams.

Straight-up, God-fearing and oh-so-fine, Germaine's ready and willing to prove his worth to Jules. Finally, she falls, hard, and almost too late learns that Germaine's keeping at least one big secret. Now Jules can either turn to her faith and open her heart to love—or risk getting it broken…

One Way or Another
February 2012

Atlanta reporter Toni Shields will do whatever it takes to get a good story. So when she's arrested for sneaking around the mayor's house, she's prepared. What she's not prepared for is getting demoted–or her run-in with stubborn Adam Bayne, director of the local young men's rehab center. . .

The first time Adam saw Toni, she was wrangling with the cops. Now she's looking for a scoop at Jacob House. Adam has no intention of letting her near his boys–yet as usual, her pushiness wins. And when she genuinely helps a teen in trouble, Adam sees a side of her that cares about more than just a headline. Soon, they become close—their attraction growing. But there's more to both their lives than meets the eye. Toni has a haunting family secret, one that is taking a great toll on her. And when she uncovers that Adam has a devastating past of his own, not only their relationship, but their futures, and their faith, lie in the balance.

Get You Good
March 2013

Sydney Isaacs has two priorities: her family, and Decadent, the gourmet pastry business they founded almost three generations ago. But both are in jeopardy when her brother, Dean, marries conniving Sheree Vern. Worse, when Dean inherits ownership of Decadent he and Sheree decide to sell it to finance his dreams of becoming a music producer—or so Dean believes…

Thanks to Sheree, Dean's plans, the business, and his marriage, soon implode in ways he never expected—leaving Sydney determined to salvage whatever she can. Her only solace is her romance with Hayden Windsor. But Hayden is Sheree's half brother, and Sydney can't help wondering if Hayden knew about Sheree's scheming all along? Soon Sydney carries out a deception of her own to discover the truth—until the consequences threaten to destroy everything she values most—including her faith. Overcome with guilt, can she make things right with her brother, with Hayden, and with God?…

Hitting the Right Note
March 2014

JJ Isaacs' dream of becoming an R&B star has come true, and it's all thanks to Rayshawn, her amazing producer--and secret lover. But as JJ enters the spotlight, the relationship gets harder to disguise. And the more she hides the truth, the more distant she feels from her faith, and from her family's approval. But support may come from an unexpected place...

When JJ finds herself helping her estranged sister-in law, Sheree, through a difficult pregnancy, she discovers a surprising ally. But she also becomes enthralled with Sheree's doctor. Simon Massri is world renowned--and scheduled to leave the country. The more time JJ spends with Simon, the more she questions her choices--in love and in work. Now she'll have to face some tough decisions. Can she make peace with an uncertain future--if her heart is in the right place?...

Made in the USA
Charleston, SC
26 July 2015